SO GOLDEN THEIR HARVEST

Susan and Hazel had looked after their father since their mother's death, but now Susan is to marry Colin, a farmer, and move to Australia. However, after Colin's Gran has a fall, the old lady begs him to take over her run-down farm in Scotland instead. Susan doesn't mind and works hard with Colin to build up the farm. Peter, one of the farm hands, falls in love with Susan, but she has eyes only for Colin. When Hazel visits Susan, she finds herself attracted to the handsome Peter, but he tells her of his love for her sister.

JANE CARRICK

SO GOLDEN THEIR HARVEST

WORCESTERSHIRE COUNTY COUNCIL
CULTURAL SERVICES

Complete and Unabridged

LINFORD
Leicester

First published in Great Britain in 1987

First Linford Edition
published 2005

British Library CIP Data

Carrick, Jane
    So golden their harvest.—Large print ed.—
Linford romance library
1. Love stories
2. Large type books
I. Title
823.9′14 [F]

ISBN 1–84395–859–7

Published by
F. A. Thorpe (Publishing)
Anstey, Leicestershire

Set by Words & Graphics Ltd.
Anstey, Leicestershire
Printed and bound in Great Britain by
T. J. International Ltd., Padstow, Cornwall

This book is printed on acid-free paper

Making Plans!

'What time do you leave for Edinburgh?' Hazel Ingrams addressed the question to her sister Susan as she padded into the kitchen in her old pink wool dressing-gown and slippers. Her fair hair was pulled up into a top-knot and she still looked rosy with sleep.

At the breakfast table, her widowed father was reading his morning paper, toying with a piece of toast. Beside him his elder daughter, Susan, was pouring herself a second cup of coffee. It was marvellous how she'd taken over the running of the house since her mother's untimely death, he mused.

Normally Susan wore a smart navy suit to her job as a secretary at Robex Electronics, but this morning she looked radiant in sky blue trousers and jacket.

'You look really nice, Susan,' remarked

Hazel, slumping inelegantly into a chair.

'And what time did Tony bring you home last night in that awful old banger?' Susan asked, seeing Hazel yawn.

'You can't be grumpy this morning,' Hazel said, ignoring the question. 'Not with Colin coming home from Australia today. How long is it since he went away?'

'Six months ... and one week.' Susan sighed. It seemed like a lifetime since she had last seen him.

Susan and Colin had been constant companions since sixth form, then Colin had gone to agricultural college. Once he'd qualified he had been invited out to Australia by his Uncle Rory who had a huge farm out there.

Susan had agreed it would be great experience for him, though the prospect of six months apart had seemed bleak.

Now she drank her coffee nervously, one eye on the clock. Beside her, Mr Ingrams' paper rustled as he laid it aside.

'Your pill, Dad,' Susan reminded him.

'What? Oh . . . yes, I'll get it in a minute. Is there any more coffee in the pot?'

'You know you've got to take the pills the doctor prescribed,' Susan said severely.

'I will, I will. Don't fuss so.'

Ben Ingrams was tall and spare, his face creased by a worried frown. After his first mild heart attack the doctor had put him on a strict diet to bring down his weight and now many of this clothes hung on his thin frame.

However, in spite of the precautions, a few months ago he'd had a second attack and was now suffering from angina, and Susan watched him like a hawk, seeing that the doctor's instructions were carried out to the letter. But she could do nothing about what she felt was the primary cause of the trouble, which was his job at Carmichael's.

The supermarket chain was well

known, having a branch in most towns in central Scotland, and Ben Ingrams was proud to be manager of the original branch.

Thanks to him, the Netherdale branch of Carmichael's was second to none, but at what price, Susan thought worriedly, as she saw the slight shake of her father's hand as he laid the paper aside.

'I'm glad you're down early for a change, Hazel,' he commented.

'I don't have to get to work until ten,' she said defensively.

'Yes, and it would have been a very different kind of work if you hadn't thrown away your chances,' her father said in a severe tone. 'I'm not happy with what you're doing, Hazel, but we can go into that another time.

'I want you to go down to Carleven to see Aunt Chrissie on Saturday. It's her birthday and I'm preparing a hamper I want you to take.'

'Dad!' Hazel's eyes were wide with protest.

She was fond of her great-aunt, but she had plans of her own for Saturday — supposing Tony was free. It was a long way on the buses to Carleven, and she might even have to spend the night there. Unless, of course . . .

'I could borrow Tony's car!' Her eyes began to brighten. 'He might even come with me . . . '

'No!' Her father's tone was stern. 'I won't have you and that young man gallivanting anywhere in that car of his. I can trust you to go on your own, but not the two of you.'

'Give a dog a bad name,' Hazel muttered.

Ben sighed deeply. It still upset him that his younger daughter was working in the office at a local garage. He was sure she could have made more of herself and had a successful business career if only she'd been willing to study.

Ben couldn't say he approved of Tony Candlish either. The lad seemed so irresponsible, encouraging Hazel with that painting she liked to dabble in.

'You'll go, and you'll go on the bus,' he said at last. 'You get on well with Aunt Chrissie, though goodness knows why. But she's the only relative we've got now, and Susan can't go, what with Colin arriving home. And I can't spare the time away from Carmichael's. We're very busy just now.'

'Every day's a busy day at Carmichael's,' Hazel said huffily. 'You lecture me, but you'd be much healthier if you took the weekend off yourself and took your fishing rod with you. It's good fishing around Carleven.'

He couldn't resist smiling a little as he rose and rumpled her hair.

Ready for the off, Susan picked up her new handbag and the car keys. She was taking the car for the day and would drop her father off at Carmichael's.

'Can you please find time to wash up the breakfast dishes?' she asked Hazel.

'I wish I could win a competition,' Hazel said dreamily. 'All I need is fifteen hundred pounds . . . We've got a Mini in for sale at the garage and Mr Telfer says it's a snip.'

'While you're about it, try to win an extra hundred or two for me,' Susan said. 'We could do with a dishwasher. Mum always used to want one.' She sighed. It was three years now since they had lost their frail, delicate mother after a short illness.

Mr Ingrams reappeared, carrying a bulging briefcase. He should let me help him with the paperwork sometimes, Susan thought crossly, but he was always so determined to do things for himself.

But this morning she couldn't be worried over anything for long. Soon she would see Colin Sutherland again . . .

Would his eyes still light up when he saw her? Would their friendship still be as warm as when he'd left for Australia?

Her mouth went dry at the thought that things might have changed between them, but then she put such thoughts firmly behind her. Colin's letters had been as affectionate as ever. There was nothing to worry about.

'Ready, Dad?' she asked.

'Ready.'

★ ★ ★

The shuttle was late! Susan waited nervously, unable to stand still. Finally there was movement everywhere and her eyes lit up as a tall, well-built young man hurried towards her.

A moment later he had dropped his luggage and enveloped her in a huge bear hug. Then he was kissing her, and her heart thundered with excitement.

'Let me look at you,' he said, finally releasing her and holding her at arm's length. 'You look fabulous.'

'So do you,' she said frankly. He had filled out and his brown hair had streaks of gold in it, bleached by the Australian sun. His dark eyes sparkled like black coals as he looked into her own.

'I've got the car,' she said breath-lessly. 'Come on — we can catch up with all the news on the way home.'

'We can stop for something to eat, too. I couldn't eat on a plane,' he went on, 'and, anyway, I want to have you to myself for a while, before we go home. I've got all sorts of plans made . . . '

A few miles down the road they drove into the car park of the Lowther Park Hotel and soon found a quiet corner in the dining-room.

'You really do look fabulous, sweet-heart,' he told her tenderly. 'I knew it would be like this as soon as we saw one another again.'

They gazed at each other rapturously until the waitress approached and coughed discreetly.

Colin was full of tales about Australia and he gave a glowing account of his Uncle Rory's farm out there.

'It's a fantastic place,' he told her as they tucked into the soup they had ordered. 'He's married, you know. I have an Aunt Nancy and three cousins

— Tom, Jill and Peter. I expect I've told you all this before, but somehow it was different to meet them in the flesh. They're really great people. You'll love them!'

'Sounds wonderful!' she agreed, then frowned as she thought of something. 'I wonder if we should have phoned your mum and dad? They'll be waiting at home for you. Oh, and your granny at Westgate Farm.'

'Oh . . . of course,' he agreed rather guiltily. 'Er — have you visited them while I've been away?'

'I promised I would, didn't I? Actually I've only been to Westgate once — that was when I got an extra day off work. It's a longish journey for one day. But your mum and dad are OK.'

'No doubt Dad's chairman of some new committee,' Colin said rather drily, 'and Mum will be organising a coffee morning for one of her charities.'

'They're good people, Colin, even if the love of farming seems to have skipped their generation from your grandparents to you. No-one would ever guess that your mum was a farmer's daughter!'

'No, and if she'd had her way, I'd be a civil servant like Dad! Anyway, forget about them — it's the two of us I want to talk about. I've got something special for you . . . '

She gasped as he felt in his pocket and produced an elegant red-leather ring box, opening the lid to reveal a pretty diamond ring which sparkled as it caught the light from the restaurant's bright chandeliers.

'It should fit you. I measured it by the ring you got in that Christmas cracker last year. It fitted you perfectly, so I snitched it . . . for future reference, you know!

'I've got the chance of a farm in Australia near to Uncle Rory's property. We can get married before we go back out there. You've no idea how he's prospered out there — you have to see it for yourself.

'Oh, darling, we're going to have such a wonderful life! There's a nice farmhouse with the property, and Aunt Nancy will love to help you fix it up . . . ' he went on excitedly.

Susan was completely taken aback. Colin was enthusiastically telling her about all he would be able to offer her, promising a much better life than he had ever thought possible, yet he hadn't even asked her if she wanted to marry him!

She stared at the pretty ring in disbelief as he chattered on.

'I know you love me as much as I love you,' he was saying. 'I knew I wasn't wrong.'

'But you *are* wrong!' she managed to say at last. 'You *are* wrong, Colin. How can you make such important plans for my future without even discussing it with me? You haven't asked me anything, you've simply told me!'

'Oh, Susan, you don't understand. This is such an amazing opportunity. I'd be mad to turn it down!'

'Then take it by all means, but you'll have to leave me out!' she cried. 'I can't just pack up and go off to Australia just like that. Even if I wanted to, I couldn't leave my job without giving proper notice.

'And you know very well I've taken over the running of the house since Mum . . . since we lost her . . . ' Her voice was suddenly choked. 'And Dad isn't so well, either. He has to be looked after. You see? You haven't even asked about my problems.'

'But surely your sister is at home now?'

'Hazel? You mean, leave Hazel to look after things? You must be joking! That would be guaranteed to give Dad a major heart attack straightaway!' she snapped.

'But you're entitled to your own life, Susan. And don't forget that you have me to consider,' Colin told her rather pompously.

'Oh, no, I haven't!' she cried furiously, tossing the ring box back at

13

him. 'As I said before, you never even asked me, Colin — you've simply told me what my life is going to be like. And yet you have the cheek to say I'm entitled to my own life? Well, that's a laugh, isn't it? Talk about being taken for granted!'

She leapt to her feet, grabbed her handbag and was fumbling for her car keys even as she rushed out to the car park, her cheeks scarlet with anger.

She had no misgivings about leaving Colin. There would be a bus along shortly — he could go home on that!

A Bouquet Of
Red Roses . . .

Hazel had only just returned from work when Susan rushed into the house and passed her in the hall, her feet beating a tattoo on the stairs as she dashed up to her bedroom.

The girl flinched as she heard the door being banged shut . . . and then she heard Susan burst into a storm of weeping as she threw herself on to her bed.

Susan felt as though her world had fallen apart. How could Colin have been be so insensitive? How could he have believed that she wouldn't want to be consulted about her own future, let alone any future they might share?

Slowly her sobs began to subside and she sat up, reaching blindly for another tissue. Her gaze fell sadly on her dressing-table, littered with brushes and make-up — she had made such an effort to look her best for Colin. In fact, she had been planning for this day for weeks, and now her heart ached unbearably as she thought about how quickly her dreams had shattered.

Her greatest dream had been, of course, that Colin would ask her to marry him, but not just yet. She had pictured a romantic proposal followed at length by a fairytale wedding, then living within easy reach of her father and Hazel. And she had thought Colin would understand all this.

Slowly she rose and stripped off the lovely sky blue suit that had taken so much of her savings. Everything had been planned so carefully, yet it had taken only a few minutes to tear it all apart. Had she been too hasty, she wondered wretchedly.

Having seen him again, she knew how very much she loved him. Surely that was all that mattered? Had she thrown that love away?

The tears welled again and she

sobbed out her misery, ignoring Hazel's gentle tapping on the bedroom door. She had no wish to talk to her sister, or to anyone else. She just wanted to be alone with her unhappiness.

As she stood outside the bedroom door, Hazel was worried. It was so out of character for Susan to give vent to her feelings in this way. What on earth could have happened between her and Colin on a day that had promised to be so wonderful for them?

She glanced at the time — it would be at least two hours before her father came home, supposing he didn't work late. But why couldn't he leave his assistant in charge for once? Andrew Fullerton certainly seemed a capable sort of chap.

Resolutely she picked up the phone and dialled Carmichael's number. A girl answered, her father's secretary, then a moment later Hazel was speaking to her father.

'Hazel? What is it — what's wrong?' he asked, alarmed.

'I think you'd better come home, Dad,' she told him urgently.

Ben Ingrams' heart lurched. 'Why? What's wrong? Has there been an accident?'

'No, but it's Susan. She's shut herself in her bedroom and she won't come out. She's crying, Dad.'

His heart steadied. 'Oh, I see. Well . . . ' He looked around helplessly. 'She and Colin must have had a quarrel . . . '

'But she won't answer the door, she won't come out. She'd come out for you, Dad.'

'Maybe . . . but I think you'll have to let her come out in her own good time, dear. She will when she's ready.'

'But it isn't like Susan. I'm worried . . . '

Mr Ingrams sighed. The shop was very busy and a consignment of goods hadn't arrived . . . He felt weariness descending on him.

'Look, I'll be home as soon as I can, I promise. In the meantime, make her a cup of tea and tell her it's on the table outside her bedroom door. You know how sensible Susan usually is. Just give her time and I'm sure she'll be fine. OK?' and he hung up

Hazel looked at the buzzing receiver and sighed impatiently. No, it was not OK! Well, she would call Tony. Even if they couldn't help Susan, his arrival would certainly help to calm *her* nerves.

Neither her father nor Susan understood about Tony, she reflected. He wasn't just like a boyfriend, he was her one great pal.

What was more, he was a very talented artist. At his home, which was a rented attic room in a big house, he had a number of paintings on the go, three of which he planned to submit to the Royal Academy Summer Exhibition next year.

'They turned me down this year,' he had grumbled to Hazel. 'They accepted rubbish when they could have had me.'

'More fool them,' Hazel had agreed

solemnly, then they had both dissolved into laughter.

That was what the others didn't understand — Tony was fun!

After Hazel's telephone call, Tony had no trouble in getting an hour off. He was working as a shop assistant at Pollock's, a stationers where they also accepted pictures for framing. With his artistic eye he was very good at advising on suitable frames for particular pictures.

When Hazel opened the front door to him he immediately asked about Susan.

'She's stopped crying,' she told him with relief, then she frowned. 'Oh dear, you don't think that's a bad sign, do you?'

'Did she take the tea you made?' he asked.

'No,' she admitted.

He thought for a moment.

'Tell her I'm here. That'll bring her out in high dudgeon! Even better, tell her we're eloping — in my car!'

'Idiot!' Hazel gave him a playful push.

The doorbell rang then, and Hazel went to open the door. A young man was on the step, clutching an enormous bunch of red roses.

'For Miss Susan Ingrams,' he announced, and the Cellophane rustled as Hazel took the flowers.

'Wow!' she said. 'Look at this!' She turned to Tony as she shut the door. 'You never send me flowers like this.'

'I've got no guilty feelings,' he retorted loftily.

'Oh, no? Well, anyway, let's hope these roses will do the trick for Susan. They would for me.'

She ran up the stairs and knocked on Susan's door.

'Open up!' she cried. 'You've got all the red roses in the country gathered together in one enormous bouquet! Hurry up, Susan — my arms are breaking holding them.'

Her heart suddenly lightening, Susan scrambled off the bed and opened the door, and Hazel thrust the bouquet towards her, grinning broadly.

'Whatever you've quarrelled about, Colin certainly knows how to tell you that he's sorry and that he loves you,' she told her.

'Oh, Hazel!' Susan felt on the verge of tears again.

'Read the card,' her sister said briskly.

Susan took it with trembling fingers and read, 'Darling, can you forgive me? Please ring! All my love — Colin.'

'Oh, they're gorgeous,' she whispered as she buried her face in the fragrant blooms.

'I'll help you find vases,' Hazel volunteered. 'We'll probably need every one we've got!'

'In a minute,' Susan said. 'First I have to ring Colin.'

With trembling fingers she dialled his number, and a moment later she was listening to his deep voice.

'Susan? Darling? Thank goodness you've called! I was so afraid — '

'I got the roses,' she said huskily. 'Thank you.'

'Oh, Susan, can you ever forgive me

for springing all my plans on you like that?' he asked. 'I was just so excited. I guess I got a bit carried away. It was thoughtless not to ask you. I should have known not to buy that ring, too,' he said apologetically.

'It was my fault, too, Colin,' she told him. 'I reacted far too hastily. I didn't even gave myself a chance to think.'

'Look, I've got to see you,' he said urgently. 'Can we meet somewhere — right away?'

She thought for a moment.

'How about the ash tree down at the river? You know the place? Where we used to catch minnows and tadpoles? Remember?'

'How could I forget?' he murmured tenderly.

★　★　★

The river ran shallow near the old ash tree, with one or two salmon pools where it eddied and swayed. Trees and shrubs lined the banks on either side.

23

Colin was already there when Susan arrived. She flew into his arms and they clung together.

'I'm sorry,' she whispered. 'Nothing else matters if you really love me, and you do, don't you?'

'I've always loved you and always will,' said Colin, kissing her fiercely. 'Oh, darling, I thought I'd lost you and I couldn't bear that, I just couldn't.'

'I didn't give myself time to think,' Susan said softly.

'No, it was my fault. I was only seeing things my way. It was selfish to go making all those plans without asking you how you felt about them. It's just — I always imagined you beside me. None of it would mean a thing to me if you weren't with me. We'll just have to start afresh now — '

'No,' Susan interrupted. 'If going back to Australia is what you really want, then I'll go along with it. I — I'll just have to sort out my own problems somehow . . . '

They sat down in the shade of the

ash tree and her heart was at ease as she was cradled in his arms. Nothing else mattered except their love for each other. She knew that now, was sure of it above all else after the misery of believing she had lost him.

'I'll change this ring for one of *your* choice,' Colin said, producing the little ring box from his pocket.

'Oh no, I love it, really!' Susan assured him. 'It's exactly what I'd have chosen!'

'Really?'

'Really!'

She watched tenderly as he lifted her hand and slipped the ring on to her finger. It fitted perfectly and she twisted her hand this way and that, admiring the diamonds as they sparkled in the sunlight.

'It's beautiful,' she breathed.

He drew her to him, kissing her passionately.

'I need you beside me, Susan. You don't know how I've longed to come home to you. And I'll always look after you, I promise. Let's get married soon, sweetheart! I know we'll be happy. You'll always come first with me.'

'And you with me,' she vowed.

A breeze stirred the trees and a tendril of hair fluttered against her cheek. Often she was to look back on this moment during the months ahead, and realise that it had been the happiest of her life.

'Come on — let's go home and tell everyone,' Colin said. 'I'll have to speak to your dad, of course, but I know my parents will be pleased. They're always on at me to settle down.' His voice had a slightly ironic ring. 'How do you think your dad will take it?' he asked, suddenly anxious.

'He'll be happy for us,' Susan assured him simply.

There would be problems, but she refused to worry about them now.

Colin helped her to her feet and they stood clasped in one another's arms for a moment, then, hand in hand, they walked up a grassy bank to the path which skirted the river, and made their way home.

* ★ ★

Hazel was almost as excited as Susan about the engagement, and if Mr Ingrams' eyes darkened for a moment at the prospect of losing his elder daughter, especially as she and Colin planned to live so far away, he quickly forced it to the back of his mind and showed only delight in their happiness.

'I shan't leave you until I feel you can manage without me, Dad,' she insisted.

'I'm not a senile old man,' Ben Ingrams assured her, grinning. 'You must live your own life, my dear, and have your own happiness. You've made a fine choice — Colin's a good chap, he'll look after you. That's all that matters.'

'I wonder what it'll be like living in Australia,' Hazel said dreamily. 'Will you miss home?'

Susan turned away abruptly without

answering. She would miss home more than she could say.

'We'll just have to write you lots of letters.' Hazel grinned.

Over the next few days, Susan began to wonder if her younger sister wasn't up to some mischief. She was often out with Tony or chatting secretly to him on the phone, calls which were mysteriously ended the moment she appeared.

'I'm sure she's up to something,' Susan confided to her father. 'Have you any idea what's up her sleeve? She denies it, of course, but she's got that look about her.'

'Hmm, strikes me she's just being her usual self,' Ben said, shaking his head ruefully. 'You know our Hazel — she's always up to mischief of some sort!'

Susan's suspicions were compounded when, that evening, Hazel announced that she would, after all, be delighted to go to see Aunt Chrissie and take the birthday hamper her father had prepared.

'Tony's lending me his car,' she said.

'He said he'd come with me, but he has to work on Saturday. Miss Grant says he can't have any more time off.'

Ben Ingrams' eyes met Susan's as he shook his head.

'I'm not happy, Hazel It's a dangerous heap of a car. But as long as you promise to phone when you arrive . . . '

'Of course I will.' Hazel tossed back her hair. 'You shouldn't worry so much, Daddy — it's bad for you.'

Come Saturday, Hazel took off for Carleven in a burst of smoke and fumes and Susan watched the car until it was out of sight, her thoughts on the future. Could she depend on her happy-go-lucky sister to look after their father properly?

Ben Ingrams looked tired when he got home that evening. The day had been humid and enervating. Now, though, the sky had blackened ominously.

'I think we're in for a thunderstorm,' Susan observed. 'It's as black as night over to the west.'

'I wonder how long it'll take Hazel to get to Carleven?' Mr Ingrams remarked, looking at the clock with a frown.

'Oh, another half-hour at least. Come on, Dad, let's have supper.'

Later in the evening, with the weather getting worse by the minute, there was still no word from Hazel, and Susan jumped up nervously.

'I'm going to ring Aunt Chrissie,' she told her father.

Susan tried not to sound too worried when she spoke to her great-aunt.

'Has Hazel arrived yet, Aunt Chrissie?' she asked brightly. 'Dad and I have been wondering if — if she had a safe journey.'

'Not yet, dear.' Miss Ingrams' voice was brisk. However, she appreciated their concern. 'I wouldn't worry too much — I know the weather isn't good, but we never get floods here. I'm pretty sure the roads will stay open.'

'Oh . . . well,' Susan said, 'ask her to ring as soon as she arrives, will you? You know Hazel — she often forgets.'

'She's probably broken her journey to visit someone,' Aunt Chrissie said reassuringly. 'She'll get here in her own good time.'

Susan went back to sit with her father and they listened as the clock ticked each second away. The time went by, but the phone remained silent.

'I wonder if she's phoned Tony,' Susan said. 'I wouldn't put it past her to ring him before us.'

'No, I doubt if she'd do that,' Mr Ingrams said.

He'd barely finished speaking when the phone finally shrilled. He jumped to his feet. 'I'll get it,' he said.

'Well, young lady?' he said into the receiver, fully expecting to hear Hazel's voice.

'Mr Ingrams?' a voice asked. 'Mr Ben Ingrams?'

'Ye-es.'

'This is the police, Mr Ingrams.'

Ben groped for a chair and sat down heavily, his heart beginning to pound uncomfortably. Susan stepped forward to stand at his elbow.

'Who is it?' she asked anxiously.

He waved for her to be silent as the caller continued, 'Is Miss Hazel Ingrams your daughter, sir?'

'Yes — yes she is,' he said through lips which had suddenly become stiff with fear. 'Is she — has she been in been an accident?'

'In a manner of speaking, sir. Miss Ingrams has been involved in an incident in which someone has been injured.'

'Someone else?' asked Ben, bewildered.

'Miss Ingrams is helping with our enquiries at present. A lady has been hurt and is in hospital here in Westport.'

'Westport!' He was becoming more and more bewildered. 'What on earth is my daughter doing in Westport?'

'Westport? That's where Colin's grandmother lives,' Susan put in, even more puzzled.

'Mr Ingrams, we're holding your daughter here at Westport Police Station,' the voice told him. 'I think you'd better come — your daughter needs you.'

'Yes, yes, of course,' he said quickly. 'I'll be there as soon as I can.'

Ben felt numb as he put down the receiver. Hazel was being held at a police station! What did it mean?

'I've got to go to Westport to see what this is all about,' he told Susan, then frowned. 'I just don't understand what she's doing there! It's so far out of her way.'

'I'll come with you,' Susan said. 'I've been there before. It's where Colin's grandmother lives ... Westgate Farm.'

'No.' Mr Ingrams pondered for a moment. 'No, we can't both go. You'll have to stay here in case I need to contact home.'

About to protest, she quickly saw the wisdom of his words and nodded.

Hastily she packed a bag for him,

listening with dismay to the rain lashing against the windows. How could he make the journey on such a night? If only she could go for him!

Into A Nightmare . . .

The rain hammered against the car as he drove out of the garage and Susan watched him speed away with fear in her heart.

The windscreen wipers could hardly cope with the deluge, and as he guided the car along the wet roads at as steady a rate as was safe, a great weight seemed to descend on his chest, a weight which was frighteningly familiar to him.

As fierce pain ripped across his chest, he did his best to stop the car. Everything seemed to be happening in slow motion as his hand reached out to the glove compartment where he kept his pills, the medication which was a lifeline to him.

He struggled to get one of the pills out of the box. The pain in his chest had never been greater as he swallowed it. Slowly he felt the medicine go to work; his arteries expanded, allowing the blood to flow more freely, and the pain lessened. But he knew he'd have to take things easier.

He poured out a cup of the strong coffee Susan had prepared for him and sipped it slowly, trying to force himself to calm down, and after a while he was able to proceed to Westport.

Hazel was almost hysterical with fright when he eventually walked into the small room where she was being held at the police station. She rushed into his arms and clung to him, sobbing wildly.

'Daddy — oh, Daddy . . . ' she cried like a child.

'What's happened, love?' he asked gently.

'I don't know,' she whispered. 'My head feels funny. I — I don't remember. I just feel sick,' she said, and a young policewoman quickly led her away to the ladies room.

The sergeant in charge, who was the

officer who had phoned Mr Ingrams, invited him to take a seat, and a young, fresh-faced policeman appeared soon afterwards.

'This is Constable Andrews,' the sergeant said. 'He found old Mrs Campbell over at Westgate, and brought your daughter in for questioning. Tell him, Mike,' he prompted the young man.

'There's been a lot of poaching about, sir, and one or two complaints were put in from Mrs Campbell at Westgate Farm, so I walked over there to investigate.

'I found the front door wide open and no answer to my knock, so I walked in and found your daughter standing in the middle of the sitting-room. Mrs Campbell was lying on the floor with a wound to her head. However, when I questioned Miss Ingrams as to what had happened, she could give no satisfactory explanation.

'I arranged for Mrs Campbell to be taken to Westport Infirmary — where she's still unconscious — and brought Miss Ingrams here for questioning.

'Your daughter just keeps repeating that she doesn't know what happened, but she does admit that she spoke to Mrs Campbell. Therefore the injury to Mrs Campbell must have taken place *after* Miss Ingrams arrived at the farm,' he concluded.

'I see,' Ben said, and sighed heavily.

His thoughts were far from clear and kept coming back to the one basic question — why had Hazel been visiting Colin's grandmother in the first place?

'Mrs Campbell's daughter, Mrs Sutherland, has also been informed. She's on her way here now, with her husband,' the sergeant remarked. 'She lives quite near to you, I believe. Are you acquainted with her, Mr Ingrams?'

He nodded. 'I don't know her well, but their son has just become engaged to my daughter . . . my other daughter, Susan,' he added.

The sergeant's eyes began to clear a little.

'Then your daughter Hazel does know Mrs Campbell?' he pressed.

'No, they've never met, to the best of my knowledge. Hazel was on her way to Carleven. I can't imagine what she's doing here,' Ben admitted.

There was a commotion at the door and a moment later Mr and Mrs Sutherland swept into the room. Mr Ingrams rose to greet them, even in this distressing situation noticing that Leila Sutherland looked far too young to be Colin's mother. At fifty-three she was still slender and very elegant.

Daniel Sutherland held a senior position in the Civil Service and he, too, looked prosperous and well-groomed, even after the long journey, now into the early hours of the morning.

There was a great anxiety in Leila Sutherland's eyes as she talked to the sergeant.

'What has happened to my mother? Where is she? You said an accident . . . ?'

'She's in Westport Infirmary, ma'am,' the sergeant told her. 'She was found with a head wound, lying on the floor of her sitting-room, by Constable Andrews. A Miss Hazel Ingrams was in the room with her.'

'Hazel Ingrams! Susan's sister?' Leila exclaimed in astonishment.

Hazel was being brought back into the room as he spoke, and Ben was disturbed by her pallor.

'I really think my daughter needs to see a doctor,' he said. 'I think she's in shock. And then she needs to be put to bed.'

'I'll see to it. I'll make some phone calls and book some hotel rooms for you all, too,' offered the sergeant. 'It *is* very late. You go, too, Mrs Sutherland, if you wish. I'll get the hospital to keep in touch with you if you're needed before morning.'

Leila Sutherland looked questioningly at her husband.

'That makes sense, dear,' he urged. 'We're both very tired.'

Mr and Mrs Sutherland were up first the following morning. Leila couldn't wait any longer before going to Westport Infirmary to see her mother.

Mrs Campbell was now in her seventies, and although she had always been a strong, vigorous woman, she seemed to have failed in health over the past year or two. Leila's heart pained her when she looked at the pale, drawn face on the pillow, the head swathed in a bandage.

'She's still unconscious, Mrs Sutherland,' the sister told her. 'She may remain like that for some time, but her general condition is stable. They say she was hit on the head with something sharp, poor dear.'

'I want to go out to the farm, Daniel,' Leila said after they'd sat with Mrs Campbell for a while. 'It's time we had a word with her farm manager. I never liked that Peter Barclay. Last time I was down, he swaggered about as though he owned the place. Oh, why didn't Mum sell up when I wanted her to?'

Daniel took his wife's arm and smiled gently. 'Because she's independent, just like you. Come on, let's go.'

★ ★ ★

Westgate Farm had once been one of the most prosperous farms in Ayrshire but now she was appalled by how neglected the place looked. Fences were breaking down, grass verges were uncut and untidy, and the farm buildings were in need of repair and a good lick of paint.

Even so, the view from the old farmhouse tugged at her heart. She loved the place, even though she had never wanted anything to do with the farming life.

She enjoyed her life as the wife of a senior civil servant, living in a charming home and serving on several community committees. She ran her home like clockwork and managed her life with grace and charm.

She couldn't understand why Colin should want to take a backward step into farming again, when she and Daniel had worked so hard to give him better opportunities.

It was with a catch of her heart that she pushed open the heavy door of the house and walked into the sitting-room, with Daniel behind her.

Inside the house things were a little better, she noticed, though quite a few things were in need of attention — cushion covers needed washing, a hook had come off the curtain rail . . .

'Excuse me, can I help you?' a voice said behind them and a young man strode in, tall, well-built and muscular with dark, curly hair and bright blue eyes: Peter Barclay, the farm manager.

'Good morning, Mr Barclay.' Leila addressed him crisply. 'My mother, as you know, is in Westport Infirmary. We've come to find out what happened to her.'

'Of course. I've just come from the

infirmary myself, but they wouldn't let me see her, not being family,' he added.

'You weren't here when it happened?' Daniel pressed.

Peter Barclay flushed a little.

'No, I was at home, in my cottage — off duty, you know. I can't work all day and all night.'

'It seems to me that not a lot of work gets done at all,' Leila Sutherland snapped. 'I've never seen the place in such a state.'

The young man bit his lip and remained silent.

'We'll be staying for a few days,' Leila went on, 'until Mrs Campbell is out of danger. I've always been worried about her here on her own, with nobody to keep an eye on her.'

Peter Barclay's eyes glinted but he made no comment.

Why had her mother insisted on employing such a young man to take charge, Leila wondered. He was obviously totally incompetent.

He was also very non-committal and even though Daniel asked him several very pointed questions about what had been happening on the farm, the young man chose to evade them.

'We mean to get to the bottom of this incident,' Mrs Sutherland said eventually in a warning tone, but Peter Barclay merely nodded.

'Of course. Now, if you'll excuse me,' he said quietly and, turning, he made his way back out to the farmyard.

Leila turned to her husband. 'Oh, Daniel,' she whispered, 'isn't it awful? I can't bear to see the place so run down. We must ring Colin — he'll know how to deal with that young man.

'Mum should never have been left on her own. Oh, Daniel, if anything happens to her . . . '

'Nothing's going to happen, darling. Your mother is a strong woman. She'll be all right.'

* * *

Young Constable Andrews arrived at the hotel shortly after breakfast to talk to Mr Ingrams and Hazel.

Hazel had slept well once she'd seen a doctor and been given a sedative, and now looked much better. Her gold hair hung in soft curling waves, but her hazel eyes still looked solemn with apprehension and she clung uncertainly to her father's hand.

Mike Andrews' bright blue eyes held more than a hint of admiration as he looked at her.

'Er . . . you don't remember anything about last night's incident yet, Miss Ingrams?' he asked.

She shook her head. 'It's like a dream — or a nightmare,' she told him, though she avoided his eyes.

'Well, don't worry about it,' he said gently. 'I'm sure it'll all come back soon enough.'

'Have you been in touch with the hospital?' Ben asked.

The constable nodded. 'Mrs Campbell's condition remains the same,' he told them.

Ben Ingrams sighed and turned to his daughter, who was wiping a tear from her eye at the thought of poor Mrs Campbell.

He gave her a moment and then asked gently, 'One of the many things I don't understand about all this is, what on earth were you doing at Westgate Farm when you were supposed to be going to Carleven?'

'Well, I want to give Susan and Colin a surprise present for their wedding. I want to do a painting, like a montage, and put in all sorts of bits about their lives here before they go to Australia. I want it to be something they can treasure.

'I mean, it'll have all sorts of things for Susan to remember — our house, her job, her tennis, you, Daddy, Colin's home and . . . I thought I could include Westgate Farm and little bits his grandmother could tell me about when he stayed at the farm.

'But when I walked into the farm-house, everything happened so quickly I can't really remember — '

Hazel was cut short by her father.

'Well, don't worry about it for now,' he told her soothingly.

The young policeman was looking at Hazel with sympathy and admiration.

'So you're an artist?' he asked.

'Yes, I am,' she told him rather shyly.

Mr Ingrams sighed again. He knew he'd have to go back to Netherdale today. He had to get back to his office at Carmichael's to attend a meeting.

'Can I take my daughter home today? You have our address . . . ' he asked PC Andrews.

'We would prefer Miss Ingrams to remain here until Mrs Campbell regains consciousness,' the policeman said formally. 'Miss Ingrams is our only witness to the incident.'

'I see,' said Ben resignedly.

Once Michael Andrews had gone, he looked at Hazel.

'I think it might be a good idea if I rang Susan. How would it be if she came down here to stay with you? She can get time off work more easily than I can. In any case, she was planning a few days' holiday when Colin came home.'

'I wouldn't mind, but supposing they want to charge me with something?' asked Hazel, the tremor of anxiety all too plain in her voice.

'How can they? You heard what that policeman said . . . you're only a witness. You haven't done anything,' he assured her.

Hazel bit her lip. 'But suppose I — I startled her and caused the accident?' she said carefully, not looking at him.

'Did you?' Mr Ingrams took her hand in his; he could feel her fingers trembling.

'Oh, Daddy, I'm so frightened,' she whispered. 'I don't even want to think about it. Could I be charged with something because I walked into the house instead of waiting for Mrs Campbell to come to the door?'

Hazel didn't want to say any more; if she admitted Mrs Campbell had fallen because she had startled her, what would the police say then?'

'Well, I can't see how you can have

done anything criminal. Anyway, I must get back to the office — I'll get Susan to stay here with you. And don't worry — everything will be all right.'

'OK, Dad,' she said dully.

★   ★   ★

Susan was only too happy to agree to come to Westport. She had already spoken to Colin on the phone.

'Mum and Dad want me at the farm,' he'd told her. 'I gather Mum isn't pleased with the farm manager. But besides that, there's Gran — she's still unconscious in the hospital and I want to see her.'

'I know, Daddy told me,' Susan replied. 'And Hazel is mixed up in it all somehow.'

'Yes — I don't understand that.' Colin shook his head. 'Anyway, I'll have to drive down there. We can go together.'

It was a fairly quiet journey, each being busy with their own thoughts.

Susan had now learned from her father the reason for Hazel's visit to old Mrs Campbell.

'She wanted the picture to be a secret,' she told Colin. 'That's so like her. I knew she was up to something but after all my guesswork she only wanted to paint a really super picture for us as a wedding present.'

'That was sweet of her . . . and it sounds harmless enough,' he said. 'My mother seems worried, though. I'm so used to her being calm and unruffled — she didn't sound like herself on the phone at all.'

Colin was to drop her off at Hazel's hotel before driving out to Westgate Farm, where he'd arranged to meet his parents.

'I'll get in touch with you later,' he told her as she prepared to get out of the car but for a long moment she clung to him, to the security of him.

'Somehow I'm afraid for Hazel,' she confessed at last, 'but I don't know why. Oh, Colin — ' She shook her head ruefully. 'We should be so happy now that we're going to be married, but instead, here we are, all tense and anxious, as though something awful is going to happen . . . '

'Nothing's going to happen, darling. Nothing has changed for us. Just as long as Gran gets better, there's nothing to worry about. I — I love her a lot, Susan.'

'I know. But don't worry — I'm sure she'll be OK.' She kissed him gently then climbed out of the car and walked into the hotel as he sped away.

Hazel and her father were waiting for her in Hazel's room, and Hazel's unhappy face caught at Susan's heart even as her father was greeting her warmly.

'I'm glad to see you. I'll have to leave for home soon,' he told her.

Susan looked at him closely. 'Take it easy, Dad, won't you?' she urged, seeing the familiar signs of tension on his face.

'I'll be fine,' he assured her. 'I'm glad Colin has come down to Westport with you. He's gone straight to the farm has he? I phoned the hospital again just a short while ago, but there's no change in Mrs Campbell's condition.'

Susan's heart lurched when she saw the fear leaping into Hazel's eyes.

'She's badly injured, isn't she, Dad?' she asked. 'Colin's so upset — she's such a dear soul. He's very fond of her.'

'It's her head. They reckon she's been hit with something,' Ben explained.

Susan had a wild desire to shake her sister and *make* her remember what had happened, but she had been warned to go carefully with the girl.

Together they stood on the hotel steps, watching as Mr Ingrams drove away, having promised to get in touch if they needed anything.

'Tony's car is at Westgate Farm,' Hazel said as they gave a final wave. 'We'll have to get it back to him somehow.'

'We're probably preventing accidents by leaving the old banger there,' Susan remarked with a grin. 'Tony will just have to wait till all this sorts itself out, just like the rest of us.'

'I can't help feeling it's my fault,' Hazel whispered, and began to cry quietly, and Susan's heart fluttered with apprehension for her sister.

Quickly taking charge of the situation with her usual authority, she suggested that Hazel have a rest, and soon she had ushered her into bed where the girl fell into a sleep of emotional exhaustion.

* * *

Colin called for Susan a short time later. 'I want to drive to the infirmary,' he explained. 'Would you come with me? Dad's looking after Mum — she's very upset. I know it's cowardly of me, but I — I don't want to see Gran on my own.'

'Of course I'll come,' Susan told him. 'Hazel's out for the count just now anyway. I'll just leave her a note.'

As they walked along the echoing corridors of the hospital, Susan could see by Colin's face that he found the antiseptic smell and hushed sounds a trial, and clasped his hand tightly to reassure him.

At the ward, they waited anxiously to see the sister. Colin's face was pale, and Susan felt his grasp tighten as the nurse approached.

'Mr Sutherland? I'm pleased to be able to tell you that we think your grandmother is making progress,' she told them. 'She has become very restless and the doctor thinks she may recover consciousness soon.'

'May we see her?' Colin asked.

'Only for a moment. And perhaps the young lady will wait in the waiting-room? We'd prefer only close family to go in at the moment.'

Susan nodded. 'Of course. You go on, darling. I'll wait for you,' and she gave his hand another encouraging squeeze.

He followed the sister into the small ward where his grandmother lay, and his heart lurched as he looked at the frail figure in the bed.

'May I sit with her a little while?' he asked.

'For a little while. The nurse will have to stay nearby.'

Colin lifted one of the pale hands from the bedcover and held it tenderly in his own. He was appalled to see how his grandmother had apparently deteriorated during the months he had been in Australia. She was like a delicate shadow of her former robust self.

Even as he bent over her, her eyes flickered open, and they grew bright as she stared at him and recognition dawned.

'Colin? Colin! Aw, lad, I'm so glad you've come. You'll be able to sort everything out, won't you? You'll be able to run the farm ... ' she whispered.

Her voice tailed away and her eyes closed again. The nurse quickly took her pulse.

'She's sleeping,' she said, 'but her pulse is much steadier. That's a very good sign. I'll just call the doctor to see her.'

Colin nodded and stood up, staring at the old lady, her words echoing in his head.

His grandmother expected him to run the farm! How on earth would he deal with that?

A Big Decision

Colin's face was very pale as he left the little side ward and joined Susan in the waiting-room. She leapt to her feet when he appeared. 'Are you OK?' she asked, seeing how white he was. 'How's your gran?'

'She's a bit better — she regained consciousness while I was there,' he said briefly, taking her arm. 'Come on, let's get out of here.'

Once outside in the car, Colin sat silent and still for a few moments before starting up the engine. Susan looked at him anxiously — obviously something had upset him.

'That's very good news that she seems so much better,' she ventured tentatively. 'Does she remember what happened?'

'What? No. I mean — I don't know — she only came round for a few moments. Oh, Susan, I just don't know what to do!'

'It's the farm,' he said heavily after a moment, gazing sightlessly out through the windscreen. 'Westgate. Gran was so relieved to see me, and she seems to think I've come to take over — sort the place out. It looks like she expects me to take charge.'

She didn't know what to say.

'You know how little time we have to take up the option of that farm in Australia. And I've already stretched that time limit so we can get married here before we go back. So it isn't as though I could come to Westgate to try to put things on an even keel, *then* go off to Australia — ' His voice tailed off as they drove into the hotel car park.

'Poor Gran — she seemed so old and helpless,' he said suddenly, rubbing a weary hand across his forehead. 'I just can't ignore her wishes.'

'Did you promise anything?'

'Of course not! I had to talk to you for one thing. I learned that the last

59

time I went making plans for us, remember? It's your life, too — but what sort of life would you have there?'

Susan said nothing for a moment as her mind looked at the situation from all angles.

She hadn't paid much attention to Westgate that time Colin had taken her there to meet his grandmother. All she could remember was that it hadn't been a very attractive place. It had been raining heavily, she remembered, and that had made everything seem pretty dismal.

'Isn't there a farm manager?' she asked now.

'Yes — a Peter Barclay. I don't know much about him except that he must be totally incompetent. The place looks very neglected. But Gran seems to depend entirely on him. I don't think she realises what a mess everything is.'

He turned to her and put his arm round her, kissing her and holding her close.

'Let's see how things go,' he suggested. 'I'll see Peter Barclay before I talk to Gran again. Perhaps that'll help me decide what to do. Meanwhile, maybe you could think about it, too. It's got to be your decision as well as mine.'

'You'll be so disappointed if you don't go out to Australia, Colin.'

Susan eyed him searchingly, remembering his great enthusiasm over that project. Already it seemed a lifetime ago.

'Maybe. Look, I'll be in touch tomorrow,' he promised as he kissed her again. 'Try not to worry.'

She nodded as she got out of the car and ran into the hotel.

Secretly, she was wondering if this wasn't a godsend to her. She loved Colin and wanted to please him, but it would be difficult for her to leave her father, especially as his health seemed to be getting worse. And this latest escapade of Hazel's showed that the girl was still too young to look after their father in a responsible way.

On the other hand, if Susan were to be living at Westgate, she'd be able to keep an eye on her family. And she could certainly learn to be a farmer's wife just as easily at Westgate as in Australia. And so what if the farm itself was dull and cheerless? She would soon bring a bit of sparkle to it.

* * *

Colin drove slowly. The heavy rain had made a quagmire of the farmyard, which he remembered as a tidy area of clean cobblestones. A build up of mud had encouraged grass and weeds to grow between the cobbles and it had obviously been months since the place had been swept.

The evening milking was over and the byres had been swept and cleaned. Peter Barclay was no doubt working more conscientiously while the Sutherlands were all at the farm, Colin speculated bitterly. Now, though, he guessed he'd be loafing in his farm manager's cottage, about two hundred yards down the lane.

About to go there, Colin hesitated, gazing round. The milking was mechanised, but the machinery was old and, in his opinion, inefficient. And where was the student? Most farms employed a student, offering them the chance to gain practical experience.

Tired and preoccupied, he decided he would leave confronting Barclay until the next day, and walked into the farmhouse.

There was a pleasant smell of cooking in the air and Leila Sutherland emerged from the kitchen with flushed cheeks and her perfectly styled hair in slight disarray. She was wearing a large apron over her skirt and sweater and Colin smiled a little, thinking how different she looked from her usual immaculate self.

'Well, Colin?' she asked. 'How is she? I phoned and they said the news is better. Did you see her?'

He nodded as they both walked into the sitting-room.

'She came round for a few moments.

She even managed to speak to me, so she's doing OK.'

'What happened exactly?' Daniel Sutherland asked. 'Has she said anything yet?'

'No, not yet . . . '

'Dinner's ready — come to the table, both of you,' Mrs Sutherland said, whipping off her apron.

Colin's appetite was poor, and as he toyed with his food his eyes roamed round the room he had known and loved for so long. But now he was trying to see it through new eyes, as it were — from Susan's point of view.

He could see it was a dull room, and shabby. Something would have to be done about it. He couldn't ask Susan to come and live here the way it was now!

'Colin — Colin, are you listening?' Mrs Sutherland was looking at him.

'Oh? Sorry, Mum, I was thinking.'

'I was asking you what Gran said when she came round.'

Colin bit his lip. 'She . . . ah . . . she thought I'd come to sort everything out for her. I think she probably wants me to take charge of the farm.'

Leila put down her knife and fork.

'Oh, no!' she protested. 'No, that isn't on. It just wouldn't do. I know this place, I was brought up here, and although I love it in a way, I don't want you to have to work here.'

'I know, Mum, but . . . ' He stopped, realising there was nothing he could say that would make her understand.

'I want Gran to come home with us, Colin, so don't go encouraging her to stay here. Our house is certainly big enough, or we could convert the study and the downstairs cloakroom next to it into a granny flat if she wants. Your father doesn't use the study much now, and I have my own room.'

'I'm retiring soon.' Daniel Sutherland nodded. 'And I'm looking forward to it.'

'Really?' For a moment Colin was surprised. His father was several years older than his mother, but surely not that old?

'I can't imagine *you* being retired somehow,' he teased Leila.

'Nor will I be!' Her eyes flashed a little at the idea. 'As a matter of fact, I'm going home tomorrow. I've got a luncheon appointment with Robert Chisholm.'

'Who's he?' Colin asked.

'You may well ask,' his father responded with a smile, though there was a sudden glint in his eyes.

'Oh, Daniel!'

Leila flushed a little and went on to explain.

'Robert is senior partner in Chisholm and Hope, the accountants, but he was also provost of the town two years ago. I served with him as a councillor for three years, and now that James Lovell is retiring as our member of the European Parliament, we're putting Robert forward as a candidate.'

'He'll get in, too,' Daniel said, with the same wry smile. 'He wouldn't dare to lose with you behind him, my dear.'

For a moment Colin sensed some

tension between his parents.

'He's by far the best man for the job,' she said firmly. Then, with the sudden smile which was part of her charm, she leaned towards Colin.

'You're side-tracking me, both of you! I really mean it, Colin, when I say you'd be mad to come here. It would be much better to sell up. I want you to have a good life, you and Susan.'

'Gran would never settle anywhere else,' Colin replied. 'It would kill her to leave — after all, she's known it all her life.'

'It's going to kill her if she stays,' his mother put in harshly. 'And don't forget Susan — most of the responsibility for looking after Gran would fall on her shoulders.'

Slowly he shook his head, gazing moodily before him. He could still feel his grandmother's frail hand in his, and remember the look on her face when she recognised him, believing that he had come to put everything right.

How could he betray such trust?

What would her life be like at Netherdale, knowing that she had lost Westgate for ever?

*   *   *

Hazel had waited eagerly for Susan's return, half-fearful to ask after Mrs Campbell. Her relief was heartfelt when Susan told her that the woman had regained consciousness.

'Did she say anything?' Hazel asked anxiously.

'She recognised Colin,' Susan told her, 'so it looks as though she could be on the mend.'

'Thank goodness.' Hazel sighed. 'I think I'd better make a statement now — I was terrified to say anything before. Perhaps PC Andrews will take it. He seems nice!'

Mike Andrews was only too happy to take Hazel's statement.

'It was such an awful night,' Hazel said. 'I thought that was why nobody was coming to the door, though I could see lights on in the house. I only wanted to spend an hour there asking Mrs Campbell about Colin and the farm. I wanted to sketch some of it, you see, for the painting,' she added.

'Anyway, I pushed open the door and called out, but nobody answered. Then I noticed there was a light coming from the sitting-room, and I — I walked in. I think I knocked on the door first.

'Mrs Campbell was balancing on a small table by the window. She might have been shutting the window or re-hooking the curtain — I'm not sure. Well, I called to her . . . '

Her voice dropped to a whisper and her eyes were wide pools of misery as she stared at the young constable.

'I — I called out to her and she turned round quickly. I saw the surprise — perhaps even the shock — on her face. I think I gave her a real scare . . . Anyway, the table seemed to topple over and she fell forward. She went down like a ton of bricks. I think she hit her head on the arm of the settee or something.

'I — I couldn't do anything. I couldn't even move. I remember that the room seemed to spin and my head felt strange, as though I was dreaming.

'Then you arrived, and you know what happened then. It was awful. I thought she was dead, and that it was all my fault.'

Mike Andrews was looking at her with sympathy.

'This'll all have to be typed up, Miss Ingrams, and then you'll be asked to sign it. No doubt Mrs Campbell will have to confirm what you've said, but I understand she might be able to do that quite soon now.'

'Then will I be able to go home?' Hazel asked wearily.

He clipped his pen into his pocket.

'That will be up to my superiors, but I shouldn't think you'll be detained too long after Mrs Campbell confirms your statement. I can't see any problems.'

'I'll be so glad to go home.' She sighed. 'It seems such a long time since

I left the house and slept in my own bed. The hotel staff have been very kind, but it's not the same, is it?'

He smiled at her gently. 'No, it isn't the same.'

PC Andrews drove out to Westgate Farm after taking Hazel's statement. Colin's mother opened the door to him and showed him into the sitting-room.

Carefully, he examined the table in the window and the unhooked curtain. Then he bent down to examine the settee leg.

It was an old-fashioned settee and the castor had been nailed into a square of wood. The edges of the wood were sharp and there was a dark stain on it, which he thought might prove to be blood.

Yes, it must have happened just as Hazel had described it, he decided.

* * *

Leila Sutherland had no opportunity to discuss her plans for the future with her mother before leaving for home. Mrs Campbell was certainly improving and gaining strength, but the hospital staff insisted that great care should be taken at this stage, stressing that she must not be worried or upset.

'I'll just have to find time to come back in a week or so,' she said to Daniel as she packed her belongings. 'Mum will be stronger then and I can talk to her about . . . things.'

Daniel nodded, though he was non-committal, and again his eyes held a glint of humour as he looked at his wife. Leila was very good at organising most people, but he doubted very much if even she would be able to organise her very independent mother!

'Colin's staying on, but only for a few days,' she added. 'I've insisted on that.'

'Colin's his own man, my love,' Daniel said gently. 'Now, if that case is ready, I'll put it in the boot of the car.'

'You always try to restrict me, Daniel. I wish you'd support me a bit more.'

He looked taken aback for a moment.

'I thought I did!'

'Well, you don't. You're never very encouraging.' She sighed.

'Well now, it depends on what you're doing, Leila. I'll always support anything I think worthwhile, but don't take me for granted, my dear.'

Their eyes met, a wealth of meaning in their depths, then she snapped her case shut.

'That seems to be everything . . . for now.'

It was quiet at the farm once his parents had gone, and Colin made use of the time to find an old pair of gumboots and a duffel coat and take a walk round the fields. What he saw disappointed him — the whole place was so run down!

He would have to have a talk with Barclay, he thought grimly.

Colin had promised to make another visit to the hospital, but he stuck a note through the letterbox of Peter's cottage, asking him to call in and see him after he had finished in the byre.

His grandmother was still weak, but she was improving, and there was more strength now in the hand that grasped his.

'Good lad,' she whispered. 'Good lad, Peter.'

She was confusing him with Peter Barclay!

'Gran, it's me — Colin,' he told her gently.

'Ay,' she whispered. 'It's you, Colin. I know. You've come home. You and Peter . . . good lads.'

It was after seven before Peter Barclay eventually walked into the kitchen. Colin had met him briefly on one or two occasions but hadn't yet got to know him, and he was surprised to see how young he was.

He regarded Colin warily, but there was no flinching when their eyes met.

'Will you have a drink?' Colin asked.

Peter Barclay shook his head.

'No, thanks. I'll have my supper shortly at the cottage.'

Colin indicated a chair and they sat

down, facing one another.

'The farm's very run down,' Colin said flatly.

The other man said nothing, but waited quietly for him to continue.

'How many head of cattle?'

'One hundred and fifty.'

'What? It was never less than two hundred for this acreage in my grandfather's day.'

'So I understand,' Peter said quietly.

'I'd like to see the farm books,' Colin told him, and this time Peter's eyes flickered.

'Only Mrs Campbell is entitled to see those books,' he said.

Colin frowned in annoyance. Then he decided to change tack.

'Can't you at least get a hold of a better student?' he asked.

'What student?' Peter looked blank and shook his head.

'If you've no student, what help is there?' Colin demanded.

'None, unless you count old Tom. He still ambles up at times.'

'Tom McGill?' Colin remembered the old farm manager.

'Right. You'll know him well enough.'

'I'd certainly like to see him,' Colin said as Peter Barclay stood up.

'Well, if you don't want me for anything else, I'll be getting on home for something to eat.'

Colin wanted to ask many more questions, but instead he nodded and watched as the tall young man left.

Surely he couldn't be trying to run the place all by himself? Where had all the income gone? What was happening to the place? He must get a look at those books, and soon.

His thoughts turned to his grandmother and he knew now that his choice between Westgate and Australia had been made for him.

Rising, Colin followed Peter out into the soft evening air.

This is where I belong, thought Colin. He would tell his grandmother tomorrow that he would stay at Westgate.

Peter walked swiftly across the fields to the small cottage which had once belonged to Tom McGill, but was now his home. Tom had grown infirm and arthritic in the years since old Mr Campbell died, and had gone to live with his niece, Flora.

That was when Mrs Campbell had come on one of her regular visits to Peter's parents at Cleghill Farm, and had offered him the job as her farm manager.

She must have thought she was doing them a good turn, Peter thought. He was a second son, after all, and a second son often had to make his own way in farming, which was by no means an easy job.

Peter had hesitated at first, but his father had talked him into it, and now here he was.

He opened his desk and lifted out the farm books, meditating on them in the absolute stillness of the cottage. Then, gently, he put them back in the desk and turned the key.

Mrs Campbell's relatives would soon get fed up and go home, he was sure. The older Sutherlands were away already, and he didn't expect young Colin Sutherland to stay long either. After all, he'd never shown any interest in running the farm before. In fact, hadn't Mrs Campbell mentioned that it was likely he was going to Australia to farm?

Soon Mrs Campbell would be well enough to come home and then everything would be back to normal. Peter sighed deeply and went to serve up a plate of good, rich broth out of his slow cooker. It was nourishing and, more importantly, it was cheap.

As he ate, he looked around. Some day he would have to make an effort to tidy the cottage, but then, so many things were waiting for that 'some day'.

★ ★ ★

Hazel felt relieved when she was finally given permission to go home.

'Perhaps I should go to the hospital to see Mrs Campbell,' she said to Susan, 'but I'm terrified that the sight of me might bring on some sort of relapse.'

'Oh, Hazel!'

'Well, it's possible,' the girl said defensively. 'I must have startled her, you see. It really was my fault, even if I didn't mean it.' Hazel looked closely at her sister. 'Susan? Is something wrong?'

'What?' Susan looked at her vaguely. 'Oh — it's just that I've tried phoning the house, but there's still no reply.'

'What house? No reply to what?'

'Our house, you ninny. I've been trying and trying to get hold of Dad. He promised to ring but he hasn't.'

'Wasn't he caught up with management from the company?'

'Yes, he was.' She sighed. 'He takes his job so seriously.'

'That's why he's so good at it.' Hazel smiled proudly.

'Well, I think it's time he let up. I'll try again to get through to the shop.'

She sat on the bed and picked up the phone, dialling the rather long number, making a face at Hazel as it rang and rang. Finally a young man answered.

'Carmichael's. Can I help you?'

'Is that you, Andrew?' Susan asked, recognising the voice of her father's assistant, Andrew Fullerton. 'This is Susan Ingrams.'

'Well, hello, Susan! I hear congratulations are in order, but I'll give them to Colin — he's a lucky chap.'

'Thanks!' For a moment she grinned, then her expression sobered. 'Look, is my father there just now?'

'Er, not at the moment,' Andrew said rather carefully. 'He's on his way home, as a matter of fact.'

'Oh, I see. I couldn't reach him there. I guessed he'd be working late or something.'

'Not tonight. I'm doing his stint for him.' Andrew's voice became anxious. 'Actually I called a taxi for him and sent him home. He wasn't at all well today — after a pretty heavy session with the bosses. I wanted to go with him, but he wouldn't hear of it. He insisted he was just a bit tired. To be honest, I don't think he feels very well at times.'

'No, neither do I,' Susan said in a strained voice, trying desperately to disguise the alarm she felt. Her father was often very tired, but he must have been absolutely exhausted if he'd allowed Andrew Fullerton to call a taxi to take him home.

'I think I'd better come home,' she said briskly.

'It'd be a relief if you did,' Andrew told her honestly. 'I've been worrying about him.'

'I know. Thanks, Andrew.'

Susan put down the phone and looked at Hazel.

'We have to go home — Daddy isn't well. We'll have to drive home in Tony's old banger. And I'll take back everything I've ever said about it if only it gets us there in one piece, and I'll be very grateful to Tony for lending it!'

Hazel stared at her, the frightened look back on her face.

'He never seems to improve for long, does he?' she whispered.

The phone rang in the tense silence and Susan snatched up the receiver. Surely it must be her father this time!

She couldn't restrain the note of disappointment when she recognised Colin's voice. 'Oh, it's you,' she said. 'I — '

'I've got to see you,' he interrupted. 'I've just been to the hospital to speak to Gran, and I've got to see you straightaway. There are things we have to talk over which just can't wait.'

'Well, I can't talk now, Colin,' Susan said hurriedly. 'I've got to get home. Dad isn't well. He isn't answering the phone, but I know he's there. I'm scared that something has happened. We'll have to talk another time.'

He listened to the click as she hung up, then slowly he put down the phone.

The silence in the old farmhouse was absolute and he had never felt more alone.

Difficult Times Ahead

It was late when Susan and Hazel eventually arrived home after a rather bumpy journey from Westport. Tony's old car had rattled and wheezed its way along the road, but, as Hazel had confidently predicted, it kept going and in fact was more comfortable than Susan would ever have believed.

The light was on in the sitting-room as they drove up and they hurried into the house. Ben Ingrams, clad in his warm tartan dressing-gown, was rising from his favourite chair by the fireside.

'I phoned the hotel earlier,' he said. 'They said you were on your way back.'

'Dad!' Susan cried. 'How are you? We've been so worried! I couldn't get through to you . . .'

'I was tired, so I left work early. We'd had a pretty hectic meeting. Anyway, I came home, took a couple of pills, and I must have fallen asleep. I'm sorry I forgot to phone you earlier. I know you must have been worried.'

'Well — it doesn't matter now,' she told him, then stopped, suddenly remembering how abruptly she had cut off her phone conversation with Colin because of her panic about what might have happened to her dad.

She was aware of a feeling of irritation. So often she was worried half to death about him, yet he didn't seem to be very concerned about his own health — indeed, he seemed to be working harder than ever.

'I take that back, Dad,' she said quickly. 'It *does* matter. I've asked you before and I'm asking again — when are you going to stop working so hard? You're doing far more than you should.'

Mr Ingrams smiled ruefully.

'I've been thinking along those lines myself, so I'm taking a few days off so I can join Laurence McKnight on a little fishing trip.'

'How is Uncle Laurie?' Hazel asked,

grinning. 'He always used to bring us sweets and crisps.'

'And the odd wee trout,' Susan put in. 'But that's great news, Dad — it's been so long since you took a break. And I'm glad you're going fishing — you can't get much more relaxing than that!'

'I'm starving,' Hazel interrupted. 'I'm going to put the kettle on and raid the fridge.'

Susan followed her into the kitchen.

'I wonder what Colin wanted,' she mused. 'He said it was urgent but I can't phone him now — it's far too late,' she said, glancing at the clock. 'I'll have to wait till the morning.'

'And tomorrow I'll have to take Tony's car back,' Hazel said.

Next morning, after a night when she slept the sleep of the exhausted, Susan tried to contact Colin at Westgate Farm, but there was no reply to her call.

She spent an hour or two after breakfast packing her father's old suitcase for his fishing trip. He had arranged for Andrew Fullerton to take over at Carmichael's, and seemed to have a new spring in his step as he prepared his rods and reels.

Hazel had gone back to work, so she would be out all day, and Susan found the house quiet without her. It gave her time to think, though, and her thoughts strayed again and again to Colin — what had he wanted to talk about? What was he doing right now?

* * *

Hazel had arranged to meet Tony after work.

'What happened to you?' Tony asked when they met in their favourite café. 'I rang the number you gave me, but your nice old Aunt Chrissie — you know, the one you said you'd gone to visit — told me you'd got no farther than Westport.'

'Huh — you may well ask what happened to me,' Hazel replied ruefully.

He leaned across the table and gave

her a quick kiss.

'Anyway, that's for being back,' he told her.

'I'd better return that kiss for the use of the car,' she said, and kissed him lightly.

'I hope you've brought Herbert back in one piece,' Tony said, protectively concerned about his beloved old car. 'I thought he'd lost his mechanical wits and taken you to Westport instead of Carleven!'

'No, I wanted to go to Westport to see Colin's granny.'

Swiftly she told him about the accident and its aftermath.

'But what were you doing there?' Tony asked, puzzled.

'I wanted to do a painting of the farm to include in a montage, as a wedding present for Susan and Colin,' she explained.

'Oh, I see,' he said. 'Is everything OK now, then?' he pressed.

'I hope so.' She sighed heavily. 'But I keep thinking about old Mrs Campbell.

I should have gone to see her in hospital, but I was afraid it'd upset her.'

She hadn't mentioned her dreams to anyone, not even to Susan or her father, but she often wakened at night, sweating and sick with fright, seeing the elderly woman's crumpled body and white face once again.

'I should have gone to see her,' she whispered, 'just to reassure myself she's really OK now.'

'Maybe, but you'll probably feel a lot better as time goes on anyway,' Tony told her gently. 'You know you can always come and talk it over with me. Talking is good therapy, so they say.

'Now, let's forget all this drama — come on, let's go to the club,' he suggested.

Hazel rose to her feet slowly. Something deep inside had changed, she realised, as she followed Tony outside to his car. She suddenly felt so much older . . .

★ ★ ★

Laurence McKnight, or Uncle Laurie as he'd always been to the girls as children, arrived in his car to collect Ben Ingrams. For a little while Susan forgot her worries about Colin and helped pack her dad's fishing gear into the spacious estate car.

'Don't let Dad do too much,' she whispered to Laurie.

'Leave it to me,' he told her with a conspiratorial nod. 'I'm not daft. It was time I winkled him out of that supermarket place. Fishing, now — that's just the thing for a man like Ben. Good, healthy fishing. Right, Susie?'

'Right, Uncle Laurie.'

They grinned at one another and she kissed his cheek.

'So you're getting married?' he said as they waited by the car while Ben went to find his old fishing knife, which he said he couldn't leave without. 'I'll expect a dance at your wedding, pet. And I hope you and Colin will be happy.'

'Thanks, Uncle Laurie,' Susan said,

smiling. 'You'll certainly get an invitation when the time comes. Oh, here's Dad. Now have a lovely holiday, both of you.'

She stood and waved till their car had disappeared round the bend in the road, then she went indoors to phone the Sutherlands' home in Netherdale. It was Daniel Sutherland who answered the phone.

'Oh, hello, Susan,' he said cheerfully. 'I'm afraid Leila's in Edinburgh, if it was her you wanted to speak to.'

'No, it's Colin I want, Mr Sutherland. I've been trying to contact him at the farm, but I can't get any reply. I was wondering if you know when — or even if — he's coming home.'

'Well, his gran's being discharged from hospital soon,' he told her, 'so I expect he'll have a lot of arrangements to make. Leila had planned to go back to see to it all, but she has so much work to get through on Robert Chisholm's behalf.

'Anyway, I expect she's told Colin all

about what needs to be done, so he can hold the fort until she's free of her commitments.'

'So he'll be pretty busy,' Susan commented. 'Well, if you hear from him, could you ask him to perhaps give me a ring?'

'I'll see that he gets in touch,' Mr Sutherland promised.

As she hung up, Susan was thinking, Why doesn't Colin ring? She realised he was busy with all sorts of things at the farm, but all the same, why did she have this feeling that something was wrong?

Mr Sutherland, too, sighed as he put down the receiver. It was so quiet in the house. He had come home early to work on some papers, although already he was taking on less responsibility as his retirement approached.

The twelve years between Leila and himself hadn't ever seemed to matter — until now. Now he was aware that it might cause problems.

* * *

Leila Sutherland gathered up a bundle of papers, putting them neatly away in a folder. This conference in Edinburgh had gone well, she thought.

Robert Chisholm had spoken eloquently, as usual. His clear, concise explanation of his policies had soon won him support. Leila was sure he had taken a big leap forward towards being adopted as candidate for the European Parliament.

She turned to smile at him when he walked over to join her.

They had travelled up from Netherdale together and had barely taken time for a cup of coffee before addressing this committee. Yet, despite the rush, Robert still managed to look cool and well groomed.

He was a tall man with broad shoulders. His silver hair gave him a distinguished air and his skin was attractively bronzed, adding to his handsome looks.

They had worked together very closely for a few years now, Leila realised, as she smiled at him. But just lately she had been thinking about him more and more.

Why had he never married again after Magdalene Chisholm died? At fifty-six he was only three years older than herself, and still seemed like a strong young man, in the prime of his life.

'Come on, it's lunch-time.' He grinned. 'I don't know about you, but I'm famished. I know an excellent little restaurant not far from here.'

'I'll need to tidy up first,' Leila told him.

'You look perfect as you are,' he assured her with a smile, though his dark eyes were pensive as they rested on her, a fact which didn't escape her notice. But it was nonsense to think that her relationship with Robert Chisholm was taking on a more personal note, she told herself. It was her job to help him politically in whatever way she could, and he was no doubt grateful to her for her help — but there was nothing more to it than that.

Their lunch together was very enjoyable and relaxed, and Leila found herself confiding in him about her worries over Westgate Farm, and even about her disappointment in Colin.

'Apart from this recent trip to Australia, I kept him well away from the land all his life,' she said. 'And there's never been any farming connection in Daniel's family. Maybe that's why Daniel says now that we must let Colin go his own way. He doesn't know what farming entails.'

'Perhaps it's simply Colin's natural habitat, out in the fields,' Robert said gently. 'There's nothing you can do about that.'

He grinned at her across the table.

'Let's stay in Edinburgh another day,' he suggested. 'Let's push the boat out tonight and go to a theatre. Dancing, too, maybe. I know a super place where we could have a late supper and a dance. What do you say? Should we cheer ourselves up for a little while?'

Her common sense told her to

refuse, yet how nice it would be to forget everything for a few short hours. Daniel never went dancing; he had no sense of rhythm.

Nor did he go to the theatre very often, and when he did, he was always restless and found something to complain about. In fact, the last time she had vowed never to go with him again.

Yet Leila loved dancing . . . And it would only be a few hours, snatched out of a lifetime.

'All right,' she agreed. 'One more day. I can't dress up, though. I didn't come prepared for dancing.'

'As I told you before, you look perfect to me,' he said with a smile.

★ ★ ★

Susan was catching up on a few chores when the doorbell rang. She raced downstairs and threw open the door — and a moment later, she was in Colin's arms, almost crying with relief as he held her close and kissed her until she was breathless.

'Where have you been?' she asked. 'I've been so worried! I just couldn't reach you.'

'Arranging for Gran to come out of hospital,' he told her as she led him into the sitting-room. 'Mum organised most of it by phone, but I had to be there to see that everything was taken care of.

'We've got a nurse to stay with Gran for a few days and Peter Barclay has promised to ring me if there are any problems.'

'Your gran — how is she?'

'She's had a bad shake, but she's a fighter.' He grinned. 'How's your dad?'

'Better, I think. He's beginning to realise he ought to take it easy, and he's giving his assistant at Carmichael's a bit more responsibility now. Would you believe he's actually gone away fishing with my Uncle Laurie . . . Laurence McKnight.'

'Good for him,' Colin agreed somewhat distractedly.

'Susan, sweetheart, I've got to ask

you something. Do you think we could get married very soon — say, in about three months? And do you think we could live at Westgate? I — I've more or less promised Gran that I'll go and take on the responsibility of the farm.' He stared at her with darkened eyes. 'I had to, sweetheart. Someone will have to do it. There's only me,' he explained.

'I know.' Susan put her arms round his neck and kissed him. 'And I'll go wherever you want. I'll tell you a secret, though. I'm glad about how everything's worked out. I don't want to be too far away from Dad, so it isn't a great sacrifice on my part.'

'Oh, yes it is,' he countered. He lifted one of her soft white hands. 'I haven't told you all that it will entail yet. You'll have to help, darling, if we're ever to get the place back to the way it used to be. It's so rundown now — there's such a lot to be done. Then there's Gran — we'd be living with her, and you'd maybe have to keep an eye on her.'

'And you'd be there helping,' Susan

said confidently. 'It'll be OK, Colin, you'll see. We'll have to make it a quiet wedding, though, maybe at the end of September. Would that do?'

'That would be perfect.' Colin sighed, feeling a great weight had been lifted from his shoulders.

'I'll see Daddy and Hazel as soon as they get home,' Susan promised. 'It might cheer Hazel up. She's been so down in the dumps since the accident.'

★　★　★

Leila Sutherland's thoughts kept straying back to the wonderful evening she'd spent with Robert Chisholm at an Edinburgh club. She hadn't felt so young or carefree for years.

It was only now, as they drove back to Netherdale the next morning, that cold reality began to hit her.

She wasn't looking forward to returning home. Always, when she'd been away at conferences or seminars, she'd been eager to return home to Daniel to tell him all her news. But now everything seemed different. She wouldn't tell him she had gone dancing . . .

'Now, let's see.' Robert's voice interrupted her thoughts. 'I have to address an agricultural meeting at Millbank on the fourteenth. How about having lunch with me first? Then we can talk over a few points for my speech.'

'No, Robert,' she said quickly, 'I — I don't think that would be a good idea.'

They had attracted attention in Edinburgh. She had seen heads turn to look as Robert took her to dinner the previous evening. He was a distinguished looking man and she had taken trouble with her own appearance.

'Why not?' he was asking with surprise. 'Surely the way you feel about your own farming background doesn't preclude any political involvement with the agriculture lobby? I'd have thought that your kind of knowledge would be an asset.'

The colour was warm in her cheeks.

If he didn't understand her reasons, then she'd rather die than explain. Besides, perhaps this strange attraction which had begun to tug at her recently was only in her imagination.

She strove hard to speak lightly.

'Maybe I am being silly,' she said with an attempt at laughter. 'OK, Robert, if you need help with your speech, you've come to the right person. We can have lunch at my place, and I'll ask Daniel and Colin to join us.'

They had stopped the car outside her lovely old house and his dark eyes regarded her thoughtfully.

'If that's how you want it,' he agreed.

'Thank you for a lovely time,' she told him. 'See you.'

'See you.' Robert called as he drove away.

Leila sighed, letting herself into the quiet house, wondering if Daniel would be home. It was beginning to worry her that they no longer seemed as close as they once were.

★　★　★

Putting her mind to helping with the wedding was certainly a godsend as a distraction to Leila.

Mr Ingrams had raised no objection to bringing the wedding date forward, and even Hazel was being more like her cheerful old self, though she was still quiet at times.

'Just so long as I don't have to wear pink or blue,' she said. 'I'd look awful in that sort of bridesmaid's dress with my light hair. Tony would have a good laugh at me. You are inviting him, aren't you?' she asked Susan suddenly, with a frown.

Susan's eyes met her father's and he smiled and nodded slightly. He was beginning to know Tony Candlish a little better, and he could see what Hazel meant when she said that Tony was her best pal. They were good together.

'Tony will certainly have an invitation,' Susan told her. 'What colour dress would you like?'

'Turquoise,' Hazel said. 'How about turquoise?'

And so the wedding gossip bubbled on.

Mr and Mrs Sutherland were equally happy to accept the new arrangements, as Susan heard over dinner with them one evening, though Colin's mother was torn between delight at the wedding and apprehension about their future.

'It's ridiculous for Colin and you to be going to the farm,' she said to Susan. 'The proper place for my mother is here with us, and the farm should be sold. It's the only sensible thing to do. Don't you think so, Daniel?'

'We can't all be as sensible as you, my dear,' he said mildly, and she felt another touch of irritation. He never seemed to support her these days.

'There's another thing, dear,' she said, turning back to Susan. 'I know you've lost your mother, and I'd be more than happy to do everything the bride's mother would be expected to do.'

'Thank you, Mrs Sutherland,' Susan said sincerely. 'That's very kind of you, and I'd be glad to take you up on it. It's only going to be a quiet wedding, though. We haven't much time.'

'There's a little over two months; that's enough time to arrange something decent. I'll contact your father. He's a prominent man in this town and we're well known ourselves, so it should be a notable wedding. I'll cut down on my own work as far as possible, and I'm sure we can arrange something in keeping with what you deserve.'

She leaned over and patted Susan's hand.

'I must say I admire what you're doing, becoming a farmer's wife, even if I don't approve.'

'We'll make a go of it, Mum, don't you worry,' Colin put in.

'All the same, I don't think you should move permanently into West-gate, Colin, not until after the wedding,'

103

she said decisively. 'At least give me that. I'm going to need you here.'

He nodded. 'If that's what you want, Mum. Of course I'll stay.'

Wedding Day

How the time has flown past, Susan thought, as the morning of her wedding dawned fresh and clear. The air was crisp with that slight chilliness which foretells that the cold days of winter lie not too far ahead.

But the sun would, no doubt, be warmer when the bells began to ring at the old church where Susan and Colin had both been christened.

Ben Ingrams was very proud of his elder daughter as they waited for the wedding car. He was looking much better after his fishing holiday. More time in the open air and less at Carmichael's had done him a power of good.

Now he held his daughter's hand.

'Colin's a lucky man,' he said huskily. 'Your mother would have been so proud.'

'Oh, Dad!' Tears started in her eyes, and she hastily brushed them away. It was a day for rejoicing, not tears.

The church, lavishly decorated with flowers by Leila Sutherland, was crowded with guests and well-wishers. Both Susan and Colin had many friends and the wedding list had grown considerably from Susan's first tentative draft.

But now she had eyes for no-one but Colin as she walked slowly down the aisle to the measured strains of 'The Wedding March.' Leila and she had decided that they would not veer from tradition in any way.

'We'll have too many traditionally-minded people at the wedding,' Mrs Sutherland had decided, 'not least Colin's grandmother!'

Mrs Campbell was now in the front pew and Leila heard her sigh of admiration as the lovely young bride walked slowly past on her father's arm, and the beautiful words of the wedding service began.

'Dearly beloved . . . '

The words echoed in Susan's heart, and her hands trembled a little. Colin would always be her beloved.

Leila's eyes had also filled with tears as she watched her only son being married. What did the future hold for both of them? She felt the pressure of Daniel's fingers on her own, and for once she knew that he understood exactly how she felt.

* * *

The reception was being held in Netherdale's biggest hotel. After a splendid wedding breakfast, carefully chosen by Susan and Leila, and the speeches, the long french windows of the reception rooms were opened wide so that guests could wander out into the gardens and enjoy the lovely sunshine.

Peter Barclay had driven Mrs Campbell from Westport that morning. The old lady had refused to stay with her daughter, or even to stay at the hotel, declaring that she could only sleep in her own bed. She'd had enough of strange beds in the hospital.

Over the past few weeks her strength had been returning and now she asked Peter to help her to a seat in the garden.

'Leave me here and go and enjoy yourself,' she commanded. 'I'll be fine sitting here in the sunshine until it's time to go home.'

Peter was only too pleased to obey, but he preferred to fade into the background. He wasn't happy about the future. Sooner or later, he knew, he and Colin Sutherland would be clashing at Westgate Farm . . .

Mrs Campbell was aware of Hazel hovering near, charming in her turquoise silk bridesmaid's dress, a delicate circlet of flowers resting on her golden hair. She vaguely remembered the night she had fallen and the girl standing in her room, but it was too hazy in her mind to recollect fully.

Now Hazel hurried over and sat down beside her.

'Are you OK, Mrs Campbell?' she asked breathlessly. 'Really OK?'

'I'm fine! Don't you worry about me. Off you go and enjoy yourself, a young lass like you.'

'But I mean, are you really better now?' Hazel pressed, gazing at her anxiously.

'The noise of the band bothers me a bit. We're quiet on the farm, you see. I like to keep away from the noise. Oh, here's Colin.'

As Colin bent to kiss his grandmother, Hazel slipped away.

'You look wonderful,' he told her fondly, and indeed she looked quite regal in her grey silk dress.

'How are you, Gran?' he asked. 'How're things?'

'I keep telling folk I'm fine.' Their eyes met, then slowly she began to shake her head, and her voice dropped so that he had to lean closer to hear.

'I've got to tell you the truth, lad. Things aren't so good. The inspectors are coming to test our milk at source.

Water has been getting into it. Our yield was up for no good reason, so they tested it.'

'Oh, no!' Colin was appalled.

'I know. I can't believe Peter has done it deliberately. I can't believe I've made a mistake about the lad.'

Colin's eyes glinted. The sooner he took over as manager of the farm, the better.

'Don't worry too much, Gran,' he said. 'I'll be back as soon as I can.'

'I'm so thankful to have you, Colin,' she said gratefully.

Her anxious face stayed in his mind, even after Susan had changed into her going-away outfit and they'd driven to Glasgow Airport to catch their flight to Athens.

It was a long-cherished dream of Susan's to go to Greece, and now that she and Colin were going there for their honeymoon, it was setting the seal on her happiness.

Two whole weeks of sheer bliss, she thought. The future could take care of itself. At least she would always have this.

'You're very quiet, darling,' she said to Colin as they waited in the departure lounge. She had been chattering happily, but now she realised that he had said very little. 'We haven't forgotten to bring anything, have we?'

Her tone was teasing but he turned to her with sober eyes. He couldn't get what his grandmother had said out of his mind. If Peter Barclay had been watering the milk . . .

'I'm sorry, sweetheart — I've got something on my mind.'

'What?' she asked, her eyes suddenly anxious.

'A crisis at the farm. I only heard before we came away.'

'What sort of crisis?'

'Water in the milk. It's been tested. If it isn't much, then it could have been a simple accident, but if not, it means a hefty fine, and maybe worse. I was wondering — would you mind if we cut short our honeymoon?'

Her eyes widened. 'Oh, Colin!'

'I know it's a lot to ask, but — but this is a real crisis, Susan.'

She turned away to hide the sudden rush of tears to her eyes. Cut short her precious honeymoon, the dream of a lifetime?

Was this going to be her life from now on? Would Westgate Farm always come first with Colin now?

★　★　★

As they travelled from the airport to their hotel, Susan shrugged away her troubled thoughts.

Athens was unbelievably beautiful, with an atmosphere so different from home in Netherdale that she could only breathe in the parched air with excitement and happiness.

She held Colin's hand tightly as they walked into the hotel and felt a thrill as they checked in as Mr and Mrs Sutherland for the first time.

'Oh, Colin, it's all marvellous,' she

squealed, once they'd been shown to their room.

'So is my wife,' Colin said affectionately, kissing the top of her head.

'After dinner,' she said, 'we can go up to the rooftop terrace to relax and look around. It said in the brochure you can see the Acropolis from there.'

'Not tonight,' Colin said, taking her in his arms. 'Tomorrow night, maybe, but not tonight.'

Her heart began to beat quickly and her bones seemed to melt as he kissed her passionately.

'I want to forget everything but you, Susan,' he told her. 'Tonight I want us to be the only two people in the whole world.'

As they lay in one another's arms, Susan made a silent vow that she must always make Colin happy, as happy as they were now, whatever happened in the future. Now she was his wife, his other self, their love for one another was surely the most precious thing they had.

'We must always try to make time to be with each other, darling,' she said. 'In the future, I mean.'

Gently he wrapped a tendril of her hair round his finger as her head rested on his shoulder.

'Of course we must,' he agreed. 'You know you'll always come first with me.'

His arms closed about her and he held her close once more, and Susan felt that she would never be happier than she was at that moment.

'Oh, Colin, I do love you,' she whispered.

'I don't deserve you, Susan,' he told her. 'You're wonderful.'

Nothing else mattered in the whole world but each other.

For the next few days, everything was as perfect as Susan could have wished. They relaxed by the swimming pool and had fun trying out the local food, brought to them by smiling waiters who so obviously enjoyed the happiness of the young couple.

They explored the narrow alleyways

of the Plaka, gazed at the sights of the Acropolis with wonder, and bought small gifts to bring home, a tiny donkey for Hazel and prints for Mr Ingrams and Colin's parents.

Colin took some time to choose a brooch for his grandmother, and as he made the purchase, an anxious look began to appear in his eyes once more.

They returned to the hotel, and settled in the lounge. Colin placed the small box containing the brooch on the table in front of him and turned to Susan with troubled eyes.

'I — I think I'll phone home,' he said. 'I keep wondering what's happening at the farm.'

'Can't you forget about it until we get back?' Susan pleaded.

'I thought I could,' Colin admitted, 'but this is really serious. No, I've got to phone.'

She nodded, seeing how worried he was.

It was Peter Barclay who answered the phone, but Colin insisted on speaking to his grandmother.

'What's the news?' he asked her when he heard her soft voice on the line.

'It's the cooling system,' she told him. 'It's faulty. It was allowing water to get into the milk. The system's been condemned.'

'Oh, no!'

'I know the machinery was old, but I don't know how we'll be able to afford new stuff. They're insisting on good buildings to house the new equipment, too, so it's going to be a fine old expense.

'I just don't know what to do, Colin. It makes me feel . . . och, I don't know . . . ' Her voice quavered and his fingers tightened on the receiver. 'Maybe I'm selfish wanting to hang on to it all, but . . . but it's our land, lad.'

'Don't upset yourself, Gran . . . I'll think of something, I promise. I'll be home soon.'

As he hung up, he turned to Susan with darkened eyes, and her heart went out to him. He was being torn in two.

'You want to get back, don't you?' she asked gently.

The relief on his face pained her.

'Would you mind? It's a real crisis back there. The whole cooling system's going to have to be renewed. The present one was letting water into the milk.'

'So it wasn't Peter Barclay's fault?'

'No, not this time. In fact, he'll be having to struggle with our old system again. He'll be needing help.'

Susan turned away, thinking about all the places they hadn't visited yet. There was still so much she wanted to do. The memories of this honeymoon should last her a lifetime . . .

'We'll go home tomorrow,' she said huskily, and her reward was seeing the relief and gratitude in his tender smile.

They managed to alter their travel arrangements and by next afternoon they were flying back into Glasgow Airport. As she looked out on to the rainwashed tarmac, she told herself that she should be happy to support him.

Colin's happiness should be all she could want.

They made their way to where they had left their car in the car park and with a heavy heart Susan watched her lovely new luggage being stowed away in the boot.

They drove straight to Westgate Farm, and as they drew into the yard, Susan looked at the old farmhouse with critical eyes, noticing that the white-painted walls were badly in need of a new coat.

Squaring her shoulders, she followed her young husband into their home.

Despite her brave words, deep down she felt cheated out of her precious honeymoon, and a tiny seed of resentment towards Westgate was sown. She would have to learn to love the place, it would be her home, but it would be a long time before she felt she belonged . . .

*　*　*

Hazel woke, heavy-eyed, as the alarm clock shrilled beside her bed, knowing

118

that she couldn't allow herself the luxury of another five minutes. She had to make coffee and cook breakfast for her father; tasks which had once fallen to Susan.

How quiet it was in the house without Susan, and what a lot of jobs there were to be done! Hazel had always believed they shared the chores, but now she was finding out that it was easier to put the clothes in the washing machine than to iron them all afterwards, and easier to vacuum the floor and dust the furniture than to clean up the kitchen and bathroom.

Ben eyed his daughter when he came down to breakfast, noting her lack of sparkle without surprise. His daughters had been very close all their lives, so it was bound to be hard on Hazel now Susan had left home. In fact, he, too, was missing his elder daughter deeply.

As a car backfired outside, Hazel's hand jerked and she slopped the coffee she was pouring into the saucer.

Her father smiled gently as he began to mop it up.

'Goodness — your nerves must be bad! You're probably just tired. We'll have to see about organising a new routine so you don't have so much to do. I could help you a bit more around here. Or you could give up your job — we'd manage quite well, you know.'

'Oh, no, I like being independent, Dad,' she protested. 'And I like my job.'

'Well, we'll see,' he said lightly.

She *was* tired though. In fact, she felt bone weary when she met Tony that evening having had a particularly busy day catching up on work in the office. They decided to go back to his flat instead of going out clubbing.

The place was in its usual state of organised chaos, with paintings, easels and a long, flat table at one end, and the barest domestic essentials at the other.

Hazel sat on the bed while Tony made coffee, and told him about what her father had said.

'But I don't want to give up my job,' she told him. 'I know it doesn't seem like much but it's money I earn myself — I don't want to be dependent on Dad.'

'Can't you stay at home and paint?' he asked. 'You'll never get commissions if you use up all your time doing other things.'

'You're a fine one to talk!'

'What do you mean? Pollock's is an ideal place for me to work. I often get commissions from people coming in to look at pictures. Besides, Miss Grant loves me.' He grinned.

'I hope you'll both be very happy!' Hazel quipped.

'Here, have some of my best coffee — it'll put new heart into you. I don't suppose you'd be interested in doing two water colours, a view of the old castle and the town hall? They've been commissioned as a gift for someone leaving Netherdale, and I'm not happy doing water colours.'

'I don't know — I'm sure they wouldn't be good enough.' Hazel, though she enjoyed painting, had little confidence in her own ability.

'Come on, it's a challenge. Go for it!'

'Oh, Tony, do you really think I should?'

She thought for a moment, then nodded. 'You're right — it's time I got back to my painting. I've neglected it for far too long. So OK, I'll have a bash. I'll give you some samples to show your customers what I can do.'

Tony sat down beside her and put his arms round her, gently nuzzling her neck. But as he began to kiss her with growing passion, she pushed him away.

'No, Tony. Not now, please. I'm so tired . . . '

'OK, I'll take you home,' he said softly, concerned at how unhappy she had seemed since Susan's wedding, he hadn't realised how badly she would miss her sister.

* * *

Leila Sutherland looked at her husband across the breakfast table, watching as he turned over the pages of his morning paper. In another week this familiar pattern would change completely. The routine of so many years would be gone.

'Friday evening then, Daniel?' she asked. 'Friday the sixteenth?'

'Right.' He laid his paper aside. 'My colleagues want to give us a small dinner party at the Portland Hotel, and I gather that a retirement presentation will be made.'

'I wonder if I should get myself a new dress?' she mused.

'Yes, why not?' Daniel agreed.

However, as she sat beside him at his retirement dinner and looked around at his somewhat staid colleagues, she wondered if perhaps she shouldn't have chosen something quite so glamorous.

He had been presented with a lovely carriage clock, and the new golf clubs he had coveted for some time.

'I understand many men find it difficult to come to terms with their retirement,' he was saying in his speech, 'and I confess I won't find it easy to part company with all my good friends and colleagues. However, I hope we'll meet often on the golf course where, of course, my new clubs will soon make me something of a champion!

'As to my retirement, I must say I'm looking forward to that. I'm sure my wife and I will find lots of things to do with our time.'

Leila surveyed the beautiful bouquet of flowers which had been presented to her, joining in the laughter when one of the party remarked that he certainly wouldn't mind retiring if he could spend his time with such a glamorous wife.

Things were going to be much more difficult for her from now on, Leila was suddenly realising. It had always been handy to use her own home for committee meetings, for the Red Cross, the Inner Wheel and the Arts Society. Now it would be far less convenient with Daniel wandering in and out. In fact, she might even have to resign from some of the committees, she mused.

Her political life, though, was quite separate. She considered being secretary of the campaign to elect Robert Chisholm as the next local Euro MP as most worthwhile, and it wasn't something she was about to give up.

She knew Daniel wanted them to do things together now that he had retired, and he'd even suggested that she might like to take up golf, but she shuddered at the thought. She could hardly think of a thing that would be a greater waste of her time!

She sat listening to the speeches, trying hard to join in the appreciation, but she felt cut off. She was only fifty-three, far from retirement age. She still had so much to do with each day.

Daniel was happy and relaxed as they drove home from the dinner.

'I'll miss my colleagues,' he confessed, 'but it was certainly a good evening. I never thought they'd buy those wonderful clubs! That was so generous. I knew about the clock, of course. As for you, you looked stunning, my sweet. I was very proud of you.'

'Thank you, Daniel,' she said quietly.

As she stepped from the car, she could hear the phone ringing inside the house.

'I'll run and get that,' she said, hurrying with her key for the door. 'It may be Colin. I told him how cross I was with him for cutting short his honeymoon. Poor Susan! But he wouldn't say why they'd come back early. He said he'd phone back.'

She rushed in to answer the telephone, fully expecting to hear her son's voice, so it was quite a surprise to recognise the deep voice of Robert Chisholm.

'I was just about to give up,' he told her, laughing.

'Sorry! We've just got back from Daniel's retirement dinner. I thought you might be Colin.'

'Disappointed?' he asked teasingly.

'Of course not. I'm always glad to

126

hear from you,' she answered smoothly.

'I hope you'll be equally pleased when I tell you why I'm ringing. I've just heard that they want us to attend yet another meeting in Edinburgh. It's important, apparently. And it may run to two days again.

'We'd have to leave on Tuesday morning. You'll probably get the information by post, but as it's such short notice, I thought I'd better ring.'

Leila was unprepared for the rush of excitement that filled her heart. She loved the cut and thrust of political arguments and was beginning to acquire, through Robert, a growing knowledge of all the many aspects of government, local, central and European. And the more she learned, the more fascinating it became.

'I'd love that, Robert,' she said warmly.

'Good. And don't forget to pack a party dress this time,' he teased her.

'I won't,' she returned, glad after all that she had bought the lovely new gown for Daniel's retirement dinner.

'I'll pick you up at ten on Tuesday morning, then. 'Bye.'

''Bye, Robert,' she said softly, and put down the receiver.

She turned to find Daniel watching her.

'And what has Colin got to say for himself?' he asked casually.

'It — it wasn't Colin,' she admitted.

He looked at her glowing face and shining eyes, and pain began to gnaw at his heart.

'No, I can see it wasn't,' he whispered, turning away.

Leila scarcely heard him. Her thoughts were already busy with plans and preparations for the trip.

'Like a drink?' Daniel asked.

She shook her head. 'No, I think I'll just go on up and take off this new dress. I've got to go to Edinburgh on Tuesday and I want to take it with me. Robert will pick me up in the morning.'

'I see,' Daniel replied heavily.

* * *

Hazel was still struggling with her painting of the town hall when Laurence McKnight called round.

'Uncle Laurie!' she cried, pleased to see him. 'Are you and Daddy going fishing again?'

'That's the idea,' he said, grinning. 'It's getting near the end of the season, so we might as well enjoy the last of it. Where is he?'

'In the sitting-room, watching the news on TV. My hands are all paint or I'd take you in.'

'Can I look?' Laurence tried to peep at the picture she was working on, but she stepped in front of it, colouring faintly.

'I — I'd rather you didn't. It just isn't coming right yet.'

It was an awful painting, she thought, as she looked at it again. She wanted to tear it up.

This was her third attempt and it still wasn't working. Something had gone out of her — that elusive, special 'something' which dictated the quality of her work. But had it gone for ever? Or was it just a temporary phase, brought about by everything that had been happening in her life lately?

She admitted that she was worried about Susan. She knew all wasn't well with her sister, and it had come as quite a shock to hear her honeymoon had been cut short, that precious time that marked the gateway to her new life with Colin.

'We had a bit of a crisis at the farm,' Susan told her flatly when they spoke on the phone.

'But what about all the crises that must have blown up while Colin was working in Australia last year? They must have sorted them out without him, mustn't they?' Hazel pointed out belligerently, voicing the thought that Susan hadn't allowed herself to think.

'The difference is that Colin knew about this problem,' Susan explained, as she had explained it so often to herself in her quiet, brooding moments. 'So he had to come home.'

'But, Susan! Your honeymoon! And you were so looking forward to Greece!'

'Oh, we'll go again sometime,' Susan replied airily, though her heart was heavy. 'There's always another day.'

And another crisis, Hazel thought as she hung up. Farming was a closed book to her, and it must be the same for Susan, she thought sympathetically.

The memory of her sister's tremulous voice was fretting away in her mind as she tackled the water colours for Tony. If only she could have done a satisfying painting, then she might feel better.

She heard her father and Uncle Laurie getting kitted out in their fishing gear to walk down to the local river. They seemed to do more talking than catching, thought Hazel, with a gentle smile.

'The season'll soon be over,' Ben Ingrams was saying rather regretfully. 'I should have done a bit more fishing earlier in the year.'

'Ay, we'll miss it,' Laurence Mc-Knight agreed. 'Ben . . . how are things

131

with you at the supermarket these days? You've been there a long time now.'

'Since I was little more than a boy,' Mr Ingrams agreed. 'And I've seen some changes in the place, I can tell you. I'm getting on OK though, I suppose.'

'You never feel like a change?' Laurence pressed.

'Not at my age. Oh, it's hard work sometimes, I'll grant you that, but I'm passing more on to my assistant, young Fullerton, now. He's smarter than I gave him credit for.'

'But suppose an opportunity to change jobs came up?' Laurence persisted, and Ben looked at him suspiciously.

'What are you getting at? What sort of opportunity? What were you thinking of, Laurence?'

'Oh, nothing,' the other man said quickly. 'Just talking. Just wondering about your feelings.'

'The only change for me would be going fishing all day,' Ben joked.

Life On The Farm

Some evenings Susan wondered why there weren't more hours in the day, then the next morning it would seem to her that every day was an eternity.

Mrs Campbell had been so pleased and relieved to see them home and she really had done her best to make Susan feel welcome, but the running of the farm was paramount for her and she and Colin had quickly got into a discussion about its future.

'We need new dairy equipment,' she said sadly. 'That's what they say. And new buildings to house it all. Where are we going to get the capital, Colin?'

He nodded and gazed at her intently.

'Gran, you've got to see Peter Barclay and tell him you're transferring the books to me. He can stay, but he's to work with me. I can't tolerate him being the farm manager and telling me what to do.'

'Ay, all right,' she agreed. 'Tell him to do it your way, Colin.'

'No, Gran, you have to tell him. He won't take it from me.'

She sighed, still hesitating.

'He's been a good lad, has Peter,' she mused. 'His father and your grandfather were best friends from boys. Thomas was always over at Cleghill and Davey's still farming there with Neil, Peter's older brother. I've known the boys since they were in their prams. Peter has done his best here, Colin.'

'I realise that, Gran, believe me, I do. But it's been far too much for him. And I don't understand what went wrong in the first place. It looks like lack of capital, but how could that be? This was always such a prosperous farm.'

The woman looked unhappy, shaking her head a little.

'The accountants check the books, lad,' she said, 'and keep them right for the tax men. I know that. And Peter keeps them up to date.'

That may be so, but Colin wasn't to be swayed.

'I need them, Gran,' he persisted.

Wearily she nodded, finally giving in.

'Ay, all right, Colin. I'll see young Peter and tell him you're in charge. Will that do?'

'Thanks Gran. Meanwhile, I'm going to make an appointment to see the bank manager. If we're to survive at all, we must get this new equipment and a lot more besides. We have to build the place up. We need new thinking on all this — the kind of farm management I learned at college.'

'Well, go easy on that, won't you, Colin? We've liked some of the more old-fashioned ways here, my dear.'

'That's all very well, but we must move with the times, Gran.'

The woman heaved a sigh. If only she was fit enough to still look after the hens, instead of giving the job to young Susan. It was hard to be stuck in a chair and watch young folk struggling with tasks which she had been able to do with one hand tied behind her back.

★ ★ ★

Susan had been dismayed when she'd found that the feeding and care of the hens and hen-houses was traditionally considered to be the work of the farmer's wife. The hen-houses were old and neglected and every time she set foot in them she spared a thought for her elegant, beautiful mother-in-law. No wonder Leila Sutherland's nose wrinkled with distaste when she talked about life on the farm!

Never used to doing anything like this kind of work, Susan struggled hard to cope with all her new duties, and early one evening she was grateful to find Peter Barclay by her side, lifting the heavy bucket of hen food.

'I'll do that, Mrs Sutherland,' he said. 'It's too heavy for you.'

'I'll have to develop bigger muscles,' she said with a laugh.

'It isn't a job for a young lady like you,' he said roughly. 'I'd try to take it on, but . . .'

'But you've got too much to do already,' she returned. 'I know what it's like. Don't worry, I'll learn.'

He stood staring at her in the gloaming, then he turned away, carrying the bucket, and she had no choice but to follow him.

'There,' he said, when the hens had been fed. 'Try to take it easy and do what you can. No use killing yourself.'

'Is that your maxim?' she asked lightly.

For a moment his eyes flickered, then he smiled.

'No, I can't afford to be so easy on myself. Still, I'll help you all I can, when I can. As I say, it's no job for a young lady like you.'

'Thank you,' she said, 'but I promise to learn as quickly as I can. I must be a proper farmer's wife.'

His dark, brooding eyes rested on her face for a moment, then he smiled and nodded, and she went indoors feeling strangely warmed by the encounter.

Mrs Campbell looked at her kindly as she dropped wearily into a chair.

'You'll soon get used to the hens, Susan,' she said, her eyes twinkling. 'And you'll soon learn to bake and cook well, too. You'll have to! Big men have hearty appetites and need big meals. A good pot of thick broth is what's needed. I used to always have one on the stove. How about we get the soup pot out tomorrow and I'll tell you what to put in it?'

Wearily Susan nodded, ruefully thinking that she'd had no idea the life of a farmer's wife was so exciting!

Colin and Peter Barclay toiled together until it was dark. Then, before Peter went off to his own cottage, Colin managed to have a word with him.

'I have an appointment at the bank next Friday,' he said, 'so that means I must have the books by Wednesday at the latest and we'll go over them together. Is that clear?'

'Perfectly clear,' Peter returned politely. As he finished the last of his tidying up, he asked, 'Am I to take it, then, that you really are going to stay on at the farm, as Mrs Campbell tells me?'

'That's right,' Colin replied. 'It is my grandmother's farm, after all,' he added rather pompously.

Peter Barclay looked at him with unflinching scorn.

'Maybe, but if I may say so, it's a great pity nobody showed any interest in helping her with it until she had the accident.'

Colin was about to make an angry reply, but bit his lip guiltily — Barclay was right.

In the tense silence, Peter faced Colin squarely.

'I wonder if we can go over the books together at my cottage on Wednesday evening, Mr Sutherland. There's something I think you ought to see.'

* * *

The first thing Colin noticed was how badly in need of modernisation the cottage was, but at least the place was clean and comfortable. A log fire blazed cheerfully in the grate and a tray of drinks and biscuits had been laid out.

'What will you have?' Peter asked.

'Nothing for now, thanks.' Colin waved his hand. 'We'd better get down to it.'

For some time, both young men pored over the books in near silence.

'Here's where the decline started.' Peter pointed to a figure with his pen. 'This payment here.' He bit his lip. 'It — it was to my father from your grandfather, in the nature of a loan. It's a sizeable sum.'

Colin whistled as he read the figure and Peter went on quickly.

'You'll see it has been paid back, but in small amounts over a long period. In other words, the repayments did little towards putting back the capital and interest lost.'

Colin drew a deep breath, but before

he could speak Peter turned more pages.

'There's more,' he continued. 'This payment here, to Mr Rory Campbell, your uncle — I know it's going back a bit but . . . ' He hesitated and turned one or two more pages. 'And here's another — to Mrs Sutherland.'

Colin's mouth was dry. He'd felt a burst of anger when Peter had showed him the loan to Mr Barclay, but now he was completely taken aback when he saw that his own family was also involved.

It looked like his grandfather had been giving his children an advance on their inheritance. That sum must have been to help Uncle Rory set up in Australia, and the amount paid to his mother . . . hadn't that been to help with his own education at agricultural college?

Peter Barclay was looking at him intently.

'My family owe a deep moral debt to Mrs Campbell,' he said heavily. 'I don't want to leave Westgate until I feel I've helped to put the farm back on its feet.'

Colin was staring at the books, trying to collect his thoughts.

'I couldn't show you this before,' Peter went on. 'I wasn't sure how you'd take it. As I say, my father has paid the money back, but . . . ' He drew a deep breath ' . . . your own family must also bear part of the responsibility for the farm running into financial difficulties, Mr Sutherland.'

'First of all, Peter — best call me Colin, in the circumstances. And I — I think I'll have that drink now.'

Peter nodded, and after pouring a couple of whiskies, returned to the books. Colin took a gulp, then pointed to a figure.

'Your salary is practically nil, yet you're doing the work of two men,' he commented. 'That'll have to be put right for a start.'

Peter shook his head. 'I have to work off that moral debt.'

The two young men looked at one

another, and there was new respect in Colin's eyes, and a glimmer of shame, too. He saw that they were both caught in the same trap — both had benefited while the farm went into a decline.

'I want to manage the farm, Peter,' Colin said quietly. 'I've had the training and I know I can do it.'

'And I've got the experience to help,' Peter told him. 'I can't stop you taking over, since I've no doubt it will be your farm one day, but I'm obliged to say that if you come bulldozing in with new modern methods to an old-fashioned farm like this, I think you could do more harm than good.'

'I know. But you'll have to accept my way of doing things. Your father paid back his loan. You owe us nothing.'

'My father started the rot, it's up to me to stop it.'

Colin accepted that point in silence and Peter went on.

'I don't think Mrs Campbell should be told about this,' he said firmly.

'Well, we're in agreement there,'

Colin replied. 'OK, it's all up to the bank now,' he said as he turned to the door.

★ ★ ★

Leila Sutherland spent as much time packing clothes for the trip to Edinburgh as she normally spent packing her briefcase. As she folded and smoothed each garment and placed it carefully in the case, she assured herself that she was always fussy about what she wore, feeling that it was important for her to look smart.

Nevertheless, her lovely new evening gown got very special treatment, being packed carefully in tissue paper and placed in its own carrier.

'You look as though you intend to stay away for some time,' Daniel said drily.

'It's an important meeting,' she told him. 'The voting takes place soon to appoint a new candidate to stand for election. I've worked hard to help elect

Robert Chisholm, Daniel, and I don't intend to let up now.'

'He'll sail home with flying colours with you behind him, my dear,' Daniel told her mildly.

'I've left your meals in the freezer,' Leila reminded him.

'I won't starve — you do see to that.' He paused for a moment. 'You haven't asked what I'm going to be doing while you're away.'

For a moment she was disconcerted. Daniel's habits were usually quite predictable.

'What are you going to do then?' she asked.

'Oh, nothing as exciting as you, I'm sure.' He shrugged off her question. He had merely wanted to make the point that she didn't seem interested. However, as they heard a car stop outside the house, she was instantly too preoccupied to realise it.

'Oh, that'll be Robert now. Time to go!' she said, closing her case with a decisive snap.

'Have a good time,' Daniel remarked, sounding a little forlorn. 'I know it's business, but I'm sure you enjoy it all.'

'Yes,' Leila said rather lamely, then she dropped a light kiss on his lips. 'I'll be back soon, dear.'

He carried her bags out to the car and stowed them with Robert's in the boot, exchanged a few polite pleasantries with Robert, then stepped back to the pavement and watched the car until it was out of sight.

As he turned back to the house, his eyes were thoughtful.

Meanwhile, Robert Chisholm was smiling charmingly at Leila.

'This meeting is very important, Leila. I'll let you see my notes before we go in and you can give me your opinion.' He glanced sideways at her. 'I'm coming to rely on your judgment very much, my dear.'

Leila blushed. 'That's very flattering, Robert, but I don't think you need my help in that direction. I only keep the records straight.'

'You also look terrific,' he said warmly.

* * *

It was, as Robert had predicted, a tough, demanding meeting, and Leila's admiration for Robert grew as she watched the competent way he dealt with each awkward question that was thrown at him.

It was later than usual when they returned to the hotel, and she was glad to retreat to the peace and quiet of her room and relax in a warm, scented bath.

She rang home and was slightly surprised to find that Daniel was out. She guessed he must have gone along to the golf club.

The dress had travelled well, and she dressed and made up with care, so that she knew she looked her best as she walked into the lounge.

Robert was waiting for her and his eyes lit up at the sight of her.

'Leila, you look sensational,' he said as he took her hand. 'I feel quite honoured to be escorting you.'

'I'm the one who should feel honoured,' she said lightly, though she felt breathless with excitement. 'You're getting to be very well known now, Robert.'

'Well, it's just the two of us tonight, isn't it? We'll have dinner, then go dancing. I want to show you off!'

It was an evening of enchantment and Leila felt as though she and Robert were the only two people in the world as they danced together. They were so much in tune with one another.

It was late when the taxi dropped them back at the hotel.

'I'll see you to your room,' Robert offered as they tripped into the deserted foyer.

She could feel his warm breath on her neck as he reached for her key and unlocked the door of her room. He pushed open the door and as she walked in, he slipped in behind her and closed it softly.

As she turned to look at him, he held out his arms and she was powerless to resist the draw of him. A moment later he was kissing her passionately and her treacherous lips responded.

Daniel was completely forgotten as he kissed her again and again.

Finally Robert released her with a shuddering breath.

'Oh, Leila,' he whispered against her hair, 'I've wanted to do that for so long, but this evening . . . this evening — '

'I know,' she said.

As he held her close against him, she noticed that the bedroom curtains were not drawn, and she suddenly felt as though the whole world was looking in on them.

She looked up at Robert and pushed him away.

'We can't,' she said huskily. 'We can't do this. It's madness! I'm married to Daniel, and you — you've got your career to think about. That must come first, Robert.'

'*You* come first,' he told her,

reaching for her again. 'I've never met a woman like you.'

'No, Robert, it's wrong. I won't pretend I'm not attracted to you, but we must stop now before anything worse happens. We can't possibly . . . There's too much at stake.'

Slowly he turned away from her, his broad shoulders drooping with defeat.

'You're right, of course,' he agreed, 'but . . . ' His eyes darkened as he looked at her. 'It won't be easy, Leila.'

'I know,' she whispered. 'But, Robert, we haven't exactly been discreet this evening. We don't know who might have seen us out together, dancing so closely. We — we mustn't do it again.'

He sighed and nodded but then, almost against his will, his arms reached for her again.

'I must hold you, Leila, just once more.'

Then with the gentlest of kisses on her lips, he was gone.

Tears rushed to Leila eyes. She had been living in a dream. Now it was time to face reality . . .

Hazel brushed down the back of her father's dark suit, then turned him round to brush the lapels. His shirt was snowy-white and quite well ironed, she thought. He was wearing the smart new silk tie Susan had given him for his birthday, and Hazel felt quite proud of his appearance.

'Oh, I nearly forgot,' he said. 'Laurence McKnight rang to say he wants to come to see me this evening. If I'm a bit late home, you'll explain to him, won't you? I didn't have time to let him know about this call to head office.'

'OK, Dad, I'll tell him. What do they want to discuss this time?' she asked.

'Oh, probably just something routine. Now, where's my briefcase? I'll be home as soon as I can.'

As it turned out, Laurence McKnight had been waiting for quite some time when Ben Ingrams finally arrived home that evening. He had been disappointed when Hazel told him about her father's summons to meet his bosses.

'That means he'll probably be tired when he does get home,' he said morosely. 'He won't have much time for me.'

'He might be OK,' Hazel said without conviction.

However, when Mr Ingrams arrived home, he had a smile of welcome for Laurence.

'Thanks for waiting, Laurie. I'll be with you as soon as I've put the kettle on. I'm dying for a cup of tea — all that business talk, you know. Fair gives a man a thirst!'

'I'll do it, Dad!' Hazel called from the kitchen. 'Do you want me to make you something to eat as well?'

'No thanks, love,' he called back. 'We had a big lunch — all the trimmings!'

After a few minutes Hazel brought through a tray of tea and biscuits and Ben watched fondly as she placed it carefully on the table. She was trying so hard to fill Susan's shoes.

'I'm off out now, Dad,' she told them. 'Tony's taking me to a play at the recreation centre. I may be late back, OK? 'Bye, Uncle Laurie!'

Once Hazel had gone, Laurence McKnight lit up his pipe and glanced thoughtfully at his friend.

'I want to talk to you, Ben,' he said. 'I — I've got something a bit special to discuss with you.'

'Oh yes? What's that?'

'Business. A fish farm,' Laurence said bluntly.

'A fish farm!'

'Ay. I'm going to have a look at one that's coming up for sale soon. It belongs to a cousin of my wife's. I've been given first refusal on the place.'

'Well I never!' Laurence certainly had all Ben's interest now. 'Where is it?'

'North-east of here. Near the coast — Kilgordon.'

Ben nodded. 'I know it. That's a fair bit away. We won't be seeing so much of each other if you go there.'

'I know.' Laurence looked uncomfortable for a moment. 'Unless — unless you come in with me, Ben.' His voice became eager. 'It's a wee bit run-down, but it could be made into a great place. I've given it a lot of thought. There's a fish farm on the west coast which would be a great model for this one — '

'Now wait a minute, Laurence.' Ben held up his hand to stem the flow, a tinge of colour in his cheek, but Laurence wasn't to be halted so easily.

'You can't deny it appeals to you, Ben,' he said.

'No, I can't deny that. It sounds too good to be true, in fact. But — but it's come at a bad time for me, Laurie. I was called to head office today as you know — well, they want me to head a big new expansion plan for Carmichael's. They say I'm the best man for the job and I feel honoured that they've chosen me to tackle it.

'The firm's been good to me, Laurie. I can't leave them now when they've put such trust in me.'

'But, Ben, wouldn't it be a big responsibility for you?' And, more importantly, a huge workload, Laurence was thinking, which, given his friend's precarious health, wasn't exactly desirable.

However, Ben continued as though Laurence hadn't spoken.

'And there's another thing — how could you manage a fish farm in Kilgordon from Netherdale? Would you be planning to move? That's maybe something you could do easily, but I have Hazel to consider.'

Laurence McKnight looked unhappy.

'At least think about it,' he pressed.

'Yes, I'll promise you that,' Ben said. 'I'll think about it.'

* * *

Hazel delivered the water colours over which she had toiled so hard to Tony a few days later, and as he examined them critically she jumped in before he could comment.

'Don't say it!' she pleaded. 'I know how awful they are.'

'You're being very hard on yourself,'

he said with a kind smile, 'but I will say I know you can do better. Having said that, these aren't at all bad.'

'Oh, Tony! I'm so afraid I've lost my touch. What if my good work was just a flash in the pan?'

'Now, now, none of that,' he said sternly. 'You're just run down. You need a break.'

'Huh! You sound as if you've been talking to Dad. He wants me to go to stay with Susan for a week or two. He has to go to Glasgow to take charge of some new project for Carmichael's, so he'll be away from Netherdale for a while.'

She frowned unhappily. 'I think he's mad to accept a job like this — he gets ill so easily.

'I phoned Susan and she jumped at the idea of my coming to stay. In fact, she sounded really eager to see me. But in a way I'm dreading it. I know I'll get the shakes as soon as I walk into that house.' She hadn't been back to the farm since the evening when her visit had contributed to Mrs Campbell's accident.

He kissed her lightly. 'You'll have to face it sooner or later, my pet. Maybe it's just the cure you need. Once you see Mrs Campbell is OK, you'll be fine. You'll be painting like a master!'

'Or maybe I won't.'

'For goodness sake, stop being so daft!,' he said crossly. 'Anyway, if you don't want to go to Susan's while your father is away, I have another idea.'

'What?'

'Come here. Stay with me. I'll sleep on the couch. You know I won't bother you.'

'Oh, Tony, it's sweet of you, but I just couldn't. It wouldn't be right. No, I'll go to Susan's. I'll go to Westgate.'

'OK. But the offer still stands, don't forget that.'

'I won't' She thought for a moment. 'You never know — I might have to take you up on it one of these days.'

Investing In The Future

Colin was nervous as he kept his appointment with the bank manager. He and Peter had worked out estimated figures for the proposed improvements to the farm and for new machinery. The relevant books were bulging in his briefcase and Susan had made sure he looked smart.

'You look very handsome, darling,' she said with shining eyes. In fact, she was more animated than she'd been for a little while, he noticed.

Sometimes she seemed very subdued these days, but Colin usually felt so weary himself after a hard day that he could only muster up the energy to hug her in sympathy.

All he could think about these days was the farm. They needed better machinery, he thought, then he hoped that he and Susan might have more time to themselves. This loan was essential to them. It was an investment for their future.

'I've asked Hazel to come to stay while Dad's in Glasgow,' Susan had told him as she'd seen him off for his appointment. 'I hope that's OK with you.'

'Of course it is,' he'd assured her. 'She'll be good company for you. And she'll be able to help you with the hens,' he'd added teasingly, but there had been a glint in his eyes as he continued: 'It'll stop Peter Barclay from rushing to the rescue at every turn! Maybe I shouldn't leave so much to you, but . . . '

'I know,' Susan said. 'I have to pull my weight as a farmer's wife! But it'll be wonderful if we get that loan. It should make such a difference.'

She was secretly hoping some of the money might be spent on updating the old kitchen and installing some labour-saving appliances.

The bank manager was a keen-eyed

man in his early forties who listened carefully to the presentation Colin had so painstakingly prepared.

When Colin had finished, the man spent a few minutes looking at the files thoughtfully, while Colin, watching and trying to gauge his expression, discreetly crossed his fingers for luck.

'The farm is owned by Mrs Campbell,' the manager finally said. 'There's no mortgage. I remember dealing with Mrs Campbell very well.' He pondered for a moment.

'I think a loan can be arranged, Mr Sutherland, but, of course, we'd need security for it. I'll formulate some proposals which you can put to your grandmother.'

'We need the funds very badly, Mr Wilson, and urgently,' Colin told him. 'The new dairy cooling system is essential.'

'Yes, yes. Well, I'm sure we can arrange for part of this amount to be made available immediately and the rest when security has been arranged.'

With a beaming smile, Colin thanked him and shook hands, and drove home with a lighter feeling in his heart. Things were looking up!

Susan was just as relieved when he came home and told her and Mrs Campbell the news.

'It might mean something in the way of security,' he warned his grandmother.

'I'm not mortgaging my land!' she said sharply. 'Did you tell that to Alexander Wilson? He's heard my views on that before.'

'He's going to draw up some proposals. Let's just wait to see what they are. Meanwhile, I'll get out of this suit and go and give Peter a hand.'

'I'll come upstairs with you while you change,' Susan said.

'I want to talk to you about the stove,' she said excitedly once they were alone in their bedroom.

He looked puzzled. 'The stove? What about it?'

'It's an awful old thing! I just can't

light it in the mornings and there's no way I can regulate it for cooking.'

'It's always worked well enough before. Gran's always found it perfectly OK.'

'But it's so ancient! I've really got to have a new cooker when you get that loan. You don't understand . . . ' She felt tears of frustration start to threaten.

Colin looked at her intently.

'No, *you* don't understand, darling. That loan has all to go towards farm machinery. None of it can be used for — for things in the house. Anyway . . . ' He pulled on a heavy sweater. 'I've got to go. We'll talk about it later.'

As she sat staring at the door that he had closed quietly behind him, Susan fought down her anger, then morosely went back downstairs.

Mrs Campbell was staring grumpily into the fire.

'He's not going to mortgage my land, not after all this time,' she repeated, and Susan sighed.

Like any newly-wed she wished she

could be proud to show off her first home, but she knew she was actually ashamed of it. What on earth was Hazel going to think of it when she came to stay? It was all so old-fashioned — so shabby.

Storm clouds had blown up from the sea, and the rain now lashed down outside, adding to her morose mood.

Both Colin and Peter were dripping wet when they finally appeared in the kitchen that evening after finishing their work for the day.

Susan had asked Peter to come to supper and, to Colin's surprise, the other man had accepted. Normally Peter was something of a loner, apparently preferring his own company and his cottage.

He was a dark-faced, morose young man, but he certainly seemed to respond to Susan. His rare bursts of laughter were always when she made an amusing remark, and he was more than willing to help her with any task.

Now Susan served up the hot broth

Mrs Campbell had taught her to make, followed by a pot roast. The oven of the old stove was still beyond her.

'This is quite an occasion for me, Mrs Sutherland,' Peter told her.

'Susan will do.' She smiled at him and he coloured faintly.

'Susan,' he echoed, then looked down at his plate and became very intent on eating every scrap.

Both men were very tired and nobody lingered for long after supper. Peter went back to his cottage and Colin went up to bed.

Susan followed soon after, determined to try once again to get him to agree to a new stove.

She refreshed herself with a warm bath, then crawled into bed beside Colin and slid her arms round his waist.

'Colin, darling . . . ' she began.

However, he didn't respond, and she realised that he was already deeply asleep.

It was happening too often recently,

she thought, her heart heavy with disappointment. They never had a chance to talk. They never even had time for their love.

She turned over and moodily bunched her pillow under her head.

Oh well, if she was going to have to make do with that awful old stove, she was also going to accept Peter's offer to light it for her each morning.

At least Peter had some sort of notion of her difficulties. At least he always offered his help.

* * *

The train was twelve minutes late and Hazel felt ill with nerves when it eventually pulled into Westgate Station. Only a few more minutes and she would have to step into the farmhouse which held such dark memories for her.

It seemed years since she had last seen Susan, instead of only a matter of weeks, and when she stepped on to the platform and Susan rushed towards her, they hugged each other tightly.

'It's been ages!' Hazel said.

'I know, but it's wonderful that you're here now. I've missed you, sis!'

'Me, too,' said Hazel. 'It's been really different at home with just Dad and me.'

However, after the initial excited chatter, both girls grew quiet as they drove to Westgate, Susan wondering what Hazel would think of the farmhouse. Would she understand that all the money had to be put back into the farm?

As the car swept up the farm drive, Hazel was pale and silent, dreading both walking into the house again and meeting Mrs Campbell.

Smiling reassuringly at her, Susan parked the car and carried Hazel's case into the house.

The big farmhouse living-room was cosy and comfortable. Mrs Campbell was sitting by the fireside and when she saw Hazel she smiled warmly.

'Come away in, my dear,' she said.

'We didn't have time to get to know one another last time you were here, did we?'

Too nervous to hear the teasing note in the woman's voice, Hazel flushed.

'I — I shouldn't have walked in on you like that, Mrs Campbell,' she said huskily. 'I gave you a fright. I'm so sorry.'

'Och, don't you be worrying about it, lass. It wasn't your fault that I fell — it was just a silly accident. Now, let's just forget it, hmm? I'm glad to see you anyway. You'll be fine company for Susan. She's young for this job and it's maybe a bit quiet for her out here, too.'

Hazel nodded, hardly knowing what to say, though she appreciated the welcome. Susan quickly offered to show her her room, and Hazel was glad to run up the stairs.

'It isn't much as yet,' Susan said apologetically, looking round the spare bedroom which, like everywhere else in the house, bore a faint air of neglect. 'I plan to get new curtains and a bedspread as soon as we can afford it.'

'I like it,' said Hazel. She sat down on the old patchwork cover and smoothed the colourful fabric. 'This is lovely — I suppose Mrs Campbell made it. And look at that view!' she remarked, getting up to look out the window. 'Is that Arran?'

'Yes. And I must admit we see marvellous sunsets from here.'

'What?' Hazel asked vaguely. She was watching two figures make their way towards the house.

'I think this must be Colin now — and he's with another man,' she commented.

Susan peered past her. 'Yes, it's Colin — and that's Peter Barclay with him — you know, the farm manager chap I told you about,' she supplied, then glanced at her watch. 'Goodness, is that the time? Farmer's wife that I am, I'd better get back to the kitchen!'

Hazel followed her downstairs and was helping her set the table for supper when the door opened and Colin and

Peter walked in.

'Hi there, Hazel! How's my favourite sister-in-law?' Colin asked teasingly, as he gave Hazel a hug.

'I believe I'm your only sister-in-law, you ass!' she responded with a laugh.

'Well, I'm glad you could come anyway. This is Peter Barclay. Peter — Susan's sister, Hazel Ingrams.'

Hazel found herself shaking hands with the most handsome young man she had ever seen. His crisp black hair was wind blown and clung in small curls to his forehead. His blue eyes brightened as he smiled and shook hands, but when his smile faded, there was a sombre look about him.

He was quite different from anyone Hazel had met before, and she found it hard to take her eyes off him.

'Are you sure you won't stay for supper?' Susan was asking him.

'Not tonight, thanks,' he said. 'I've got supper all cooked at the cottage. And anyway, you'll want your sister to yourself for a spell. I'll see you in the morning then. 'Night, all.'

As their chorus of farewells followed him to the door, Hazel felt as though the breath had been sucked out of her, and she ate little once they sat down to supper.

Mrs Campbell's bright eyes fell on her and her half-full plate.

'You'll have to do better than that, lass,' she said, smiling.

Hazel grinned — she was bowled over by Peter Barclay and simply too excited to eat.

As the two girls washed up after the meal, she bombarded Susan with questions about him. Was he married? Where was his cottage? Did he live with his parents?

'He's so handsome,' she sighed. 'He looks ever so romantic, like Rob Roy or one of those old heroes of the Highlands!'

'Oh, for goodness sake! He's just an ordinary, hard-working young man,' Susan replied flatly and finally managed to deflect her sister on to another topic.

However, once Hazel had gone upstairs for a bath before bedtime, Susan's mind went back to her sister's obvious attraction to Peter.

She knew the girl could be incredibly impulsive, but surely she wouldn't be silly enough to fall for Peter Barclay? If so, Susan would do all in her power to prevent her young sister from becoming a farmer's wife!

Instantly she felt guilty at the thought. Was her life so hard that she didn't wish it on someone she loved?

She loved Colin. That was all that mattered. And she must put any other disloyal thoughts aside.

⋆ ⋆ ⋆

Leila Sutherland checked her engagement diary, then laid her pen aside with a small sigh. At one time she would have been full of energy and enthusiasm for organising a fund-raising bring and buy sale, but over the past week or two, much of the sparkle seemed to have gone from her life.

She hadn't seen or spoken to Robert Chisholm for some time now, and she was also having to get used to the fact that Daniel was around the house a great deal more since his retiral.

Although she recalled passing some remark about the predictability of his week, Daniel had made no reply, and she soon found herself staying in alone on Tuesday evenings whilst he did voluntary work at the Adult Literacy and Numeracy Centre in town.

'It's great fun,' he told her. 'And they're so keen to learn.'

She nodded rather dejectedly, staring at him for a moment. Something was different . . .

'Your hair needs cutting,' she said finally.

'I'm growing it longer,' he told her, a faint tinge of colour in his cheeks. He'd also begun wearing more colourful shirts and sweaters, Leila suddenly realised. Today he was wearing a rather loudly patterned cardigan over a red shirt that she didn't recall ever seeing before, rather than his usual classic navy, grey or beige sweater with tastefully matching cotton shirt.

On Wednesday morning, she watched him dress for an early game of golf and again noted the change in his wardrobe. He had always favoured the rather sombre dark trousers and expensive emblemed sweater that all his business-men clubmates wore, but today he was in white sweater and black and white checked trousers, and it crossed her mind that he looked most unlike himself.

Left alone in the house, she jumped when the doorbell rang. She wasn't expecting anyone. But when she opened the door, Robert stepped quickly into the hall.

'I know Daniel has just left,' he said. 'I watched him drive away. Oh, Leila . . .'

Her heart lurched and suddenly she was in his arms and he was kissing her passionately.

'I can't keep away from you,' he whispered. 'I can't do anything for thinking about you.'

'It's the same for me,' Leila admitted huskily. 'Oh, Robert, it's madness — but I can't help myself. I've missed you so much.'

'Nothing seems to matter without you,' he murmured.

'I know,' she whispered. 'I feel the same.'

'What are we going to do?' Robert sighed heavily. 'I'd give it all up for you, Leila. My political career — everything!'

'No!' she cried. 'No, I can't let you do that.'

She sank down on to the sofa and gazed at him helplessly.

'People will begin to talk if we're seen together any more,' she told him. 'I met a woman at the last council meeting who'd seen us in Edinburgh, and she was quizzing me about it. I managed to laugh it off but . . . And then there's Daniel. I — I couldn't hurt him, Robert.'

'But you can't feel for him as you feel for me,' he protested.

She shook her head, hardly knowing what she felt for Daniel any more.

'Look, there's a meeting coming up in London,' Robert told her. 'As my campaign secretary, you'll be asked to attend. You've got to come, Leila. It'll be something we can look forward to, something to keep us going.'

Warmth flooded her heart. Surely they could safely be together in London. There would be no speculating eyes watching them there.

'But is it wise, Robert?' she asked, hesitating.

'Surely we're entitled to a little time together,' he said persuasively, and bent his head to kiss her lips.

She could feel herself responding again, and pushed him gently away. Not here, in Daniel's home.

Sensitive to her feelings, he kissed her hand and rose to go, turning to wave from the gate and calling something about the agenda for the next meeting.

'See you then — 'bye for now,' he called loudly.

Leila nodded and shut the door, then leaned against it, her eyes raised heavenwards.

What was happening to her? Had she no control over her wayward emotions?

★   ★   ★

'That's Dad on the phone,' Hazel called to Susan, who was busy in Westgate's old kitchen. 'He wanted to be sure I was OK, and he wants a word with you.'

Susan was delighted to hear his voice but as usual her first thought was for his health.

'Are you all right, Dad?' she asked anxiously. 'Hazel told me all about the new project you're working on at Carmichael's; and about Uncle Laurie's idea, too.'

'Nothing's a secret once Hazel's got a hold of it,' Ben Ingrams remarked ruefully.

'It sounds like a wonderful chance for you to work with Uncle Laurie,' she commented encouragingly. 'I think it's a great idea and so does Colin,' she added. 'We were chatting about it last night over supper.'

'Well, it's out of the question just now,' he told her. 'I'm far too busy with Carmichael's business to even think about the fish farm.'

'It would be a less hectic life for you, Dad,' she pointed out.

'It would also mean leaving Netherdale. Have you thought about that, and what it would mean?'

In fact she hadn't thought of that. And if her father moved away, where would that leave Hazel? Their home would have to be sold. Silently she considered the implications, and in the silence she could hear how breathless her father seemed.

He had been like that before his last heart attack, she recalled, and she was suddenly afraid that he was overdoing things again.

'Look, Dad, maybe there are problems to be ironed out,' she said quickly, 'but I don't think you should dismiss Uncle Laurie's idea too hastily. How long have you got to make up your mind?'

'Oh, a month or two yet, I think,' he replied vaguely. 'It's all in the air as yet.'

'Well, think about it, that's all I'm asking. And look after yourself, Dad.' Though she spoke firmly, she knew she was probably wasting her breath. Her father paid little heed to his health.

★   ★   ★

Hazel was feeling quite cheerful as she walked out into the cool, fresh air of the farmyard. She was beginning to get to know the layout of the farm buildings, and already a new building was having its foundations laid by a big firm of contractors.

She'd heard Colin and Peter arguing over this.

'I tell you, they've estimated nearly

twice as much as some of the smaller firms,' Peter had objected.

'It'll be cheaper in the long run, though,' Colin had argued. 'At least they'll get on with the job quickly.'

Peter had also complained about Colin's scheme for new pasture.

'But modern methods of treating the land will work wonders,' Colin had told him. 'I studied modern methods at college.'

'Well, they're no use here,' Peter had replied scornfully. 'This is an old-fashioned farm and you've got to treat it as one. You talk to Tam Maitland on Tuesday when we go to the market. He'll tell you how to treat the land.'

Colin's lips had been tight but he'd nodded. 'OK, I will!'

Now she contrived to run into Peter as he left the byre and crossed the yard.

'Hello there!' she called. 'Isn't it a lovely day?'

'Pretty fresh,' he said.

'Susan has sent me out,' she told him. 'She wants to bake scones on the

179

griddle for Mrs Campbell and she says I put her off!'

'She's a very competent young lady but a lot is expected of her,' Peter said stiffly.

'Oh, she can cope.' Hazel laughed. 'She's always been able to cope. She even took over the running of the house after Mum died.'

'Did she?' Peter looked at her closely. 'Then she had a heavy responsibility like this even when she was younger?'

'I'm afraid so. Dad always says he'd never have managed without her.'

'I can believe it,' Peter murmured.

'Do you mind if I walk about with you for a little while?' Hazel asked shyly, and heard him sigh. 'I won't be any bother, I promise,' she wheedled.

'No, of course you won't,' he said resignedly.

'Where are you going now?' she asked as she followed him towards one of the sheds.

'To get a stiff brush. This cobbled

yard has been neglected, but every-thing's being cleaned up and repaired now. There was never any time when I was on my own, but now I can manage a bit of time each day to catch up on that kind of thing.'

'I see.' Hazel smiled. 'And what can I do?'

He looked at her and smiled briefly.

'Help Susan,' he told her, 'if you can. God knows she needs it.'

Why should he say that, wondered Hazel. Did farmers' wives have their own particular tasks and was Susan falling down on hers?

'Being a farmer's wife is a job in itself, Hazel,' she recalled Susan telling her when they'd been chatting one day. 'It isn't easy to learn if you're not born to it.'

Peter was using a big broom, thumping it between the cobbles, then sweeping away the accumulated earth and weeds.

'Don't you do the washing up for your sister?' he pressed.

'Of course I do,' she assured him. 'I'll go and see how she's getting on. Shall I see you later?'

'I'll be here,' he told her expressionlessly.

Hazel came upon Susan just as she was hanging up after talking to their father on the phone.

'I'm worried about Dad,' Susan confided. 'He sounds so tired these days. I think that new project at Carmichael's is too much for him, though he'd never admit it. I wish he'd consider buying the fish farm with Uncle Laurie.'

'I do, too.' Hazel said stoutly. 'But we can't make him, can we?'

'Look, why don't you go home for a couple of days?' asked Susan. 'Keep an eye on him.'

'But — '

'You could talk to Uncle Laurie,' Susan interrupted. 'Find out about this scheme of his. We don't really know much about it. I worry so much about Dad. That job of his is so demanding.

But I know he'd be miserable if he retired — he'd have so little to do all of a sudden. The fish farm seems like the ideal solution.'

'That's true,' Hazel agreed.

'He — he did mention that it might mean moving away from Netherdale,' Susan said tentatively, but Hazel wasn't listening. She was gazing out of the window, watching Colin and Peter Barclay.

'I don't think I need to go home, at least not this week,' she said as she watched.

She was gazing at Peter with open admiration and Susan's heart sank. She knew the girl had been following him around the farm, trying to talk to him. Even Colin had remarked on it, half-amused.

'Our Hazel seems to be quite fascinated by the farm,' he'd teased. 'She's never tired of asking Peter questions about it.'

It wasn't the farm, Susan knew — it was Peter, who was surely the embodiment of every fine, stalwart hero the girl had ever read about. He was certainly different from any of the young men she had ever met before, and was very different from Tony Candlish.

However, she hoped she'd quickly get over this crush and return home to Tony.

That night, lying in Colin's arms, she was glad of his nearness and his love, though she hesitated to talk to him about her fears for Hazel.

Again he was at odds with Peter.

'I've promised to speak to his friend Tam Maitland about how to deal with the farm, but it seems such a waste of time,' he said.

'Can't we talk about us instead of work for a change?' she asked, trying to laugh, and he drew her closer and kissed her.

'You know you're always in my thoughts,' he whispered, 'but I can't help thinking about the farm . . . '

She sighed, though for once her eyes were full of humour. She knew she had Colin's love.

But she didn't want Hazel to fall for Peter. Hazel would never settle down to this sort of life.

★ ★ ★

Susan shivered in the cold kitchen the following morning. Somehow she had to get this monster of a stove going before Mrs Campbell had breakfast, and before Hazel came downstairs. Both men would come in for breakfast this morning, too, before going off to market.

As she watched the flames dying out for the third time, frustration got the better of her and she sank to her knees and let the tears well in her eyes.

"Morning, Susan! I need to use the phone — ' Peter's voice hailed her from the door and she whirled round quickly, her tears all too evident. In a moment he was beside her.

'What's wrong? Is it the stove?' he asked gently, and as she nodded in mute misery, he smiled reassuringly.

'Don't worry, I'll see to it. We'll soon get it going,' he said, kneeling to the task.

True to his word, he soon magically coaxed the fire into life, and as the cold dampness of the kitchen seemed to melt into the shadows, she smiled shakily.

'Thank you,' she said with heartfelt gratitude as he rose and smiled at her.

Hazel had just come down from her room, and as she paused to watch silently from the doorway, something in Peter's face made her thoughts take off in a whirl.

Colin rushed past her into the kitchen as she stood there.

'What does the vet say?' he asked Peter.

'I — I haven't rung him yet,' Peter faltered.

'He was helping me with the stove,' put in Susan.

'Then he had no business helping you when there's something urgent to be done! You know that very well,'

Colin snapped, then turned his angry gaze on Peter.

'I've told you before to stay away from my wife's chores. She's a competent girl and she'll manage very well without your help.'

'Oh will she? You seem to forget she's no hefty farm lass!' cried Peter. 'She's a slender girl, a beautiful girl. It . . . it's like harnessing a racehorse to the plough. You can't use her like this.'

For a moment Colin looked dumbstruck, then he reacted with fury.

'I'm not 'using' her, as you put it,' he shouted. 'Susan is my wife! She knows the position here.'

'Well, you should look after her better,' Peter retorted. 'I'll phone the vet now.'

Tears were streaming down Susan's cheeks, and Colin went to take her into his arms.

'I'm sorry, sweetheart, but you do understand, don't you?' he said gently. 'This is our farm, and we have to work at it together. As soon as we get a little clear of the bills, I'll see about a new stove for you, I promise.'

She nodded. She did understand, but sometimes it was so hard.

Colin wanted her to take her place as a farmer's wife but sometimes she so longed for them to have a more ordinary marriage.

All the same, she must try not to accept Peter's help again. It was only going to make trouble between the two men.

Hazel had tiptoed away from the intensely personal scene, devastated by what she had seen.

She was beginning to fall in love with Peter Barclay. Oh, she knew Susan would say it was just an infatuation, but Hazel only knew that she thought Peter Barclay was the most wonderful man in the world.

Perhaps it *was* all in her imagination, but her heart beat painfully and tears were near, for she realised now Peter had little interest in her. It was Susan he loved, and he loved her deeply. She had seen it in his face as he looked at her.

As for Susan, at the moment she didn't see that love, but she might come to recognise it, or Peter might tell her. And what then? How would Susan react? Would her love for Colin be strong enough to help her resist the other man?

'We'll Think Of Something . . .'

Alexander Wilson, Mrs Campbell's bank manager, drove up to Westgate next day with his briefcase bulging with all the relevant documents for a bank loan.

He had already put his proposals to Colin, who didn't care too much for mortgaging such a slice of their land, but there seemed to be no other way.

'It'll all have to be explained to my grandmother, Mr Wilson,' he'd said, and the bank manager nodded.

'I'd better call on Mrs Campbell — she'll have to sign the documents anyway.'

The big farmhouse living-room looked quite bright and fresh when Mr Wilson arrived, thanks to the determined efforts of Susan and

Hazel, who had washed curtains and covers, polished brasses and coppers till they shone, and set out vases of colourful flowers.

Colin had prepared his grandmother for Alexander Wilson's visit, and now she slipped on her reading spectacles as he spread out the papers for her inspection and listened while the proposals were carefully explained to her.

'The money can be put into your account straightaway,' Mr Wilson explained. 'You only have to sign here.'

'And my land will have a mortgage hanging over it,' she said flatly, then looked at Colin. 'I'm sorry, lad, but you'll have to find another way round. I'm not going to sign these papers.'

Colin looked at her in dismay and consternation. Unless she signed the papers for the bank loan, all his plans for Westgate would have to be abandoned.

'But, Gran . . . ' he protested.

She looked at him with the grim determination he had often seen in her. Mr Wilson was also staring at him, both men uncomfortably aware that Colin had already used up the advance he had received and desperately need the rest of the money to pay for the new building work already under way.

'It's essential that we do this, Gran,' Colin appealed once more.

'Not this way, Colin. There must be another way. You'll think of something, lad. We've never had to mortgage our land before.'

But things are different now, Colin thought wearily — the farm's losing money now . . .

Mr Wilson's face was inscrutable as he began gathering up his papers, then he turned to Colin.

'I think it would be better if I leave you to talk this over together,' he said, forcing a smile, though there was an anxious note in his voice.

He and Colin had taken the old lady's co-operation for granted, in spite of what she had said before about mortgaging any of the land. Both had assumed that when it came to the bit, they would be able to persuade her.

Colin saw him to the door, then returned to the sitting-room where Susan had brought in a tray of coffee.

'Oh, has Mr Wilson gone already?' she asked, laying the tray on the table.

'There was no need for him to stay,' Mrs Campbell replied with some asperity, then she turned to her grandson. 'I told you I wouldn't mortgage our land, Colin!'

'It won't be our land much longer if we don't do something soon!' he returned bitterly.

Then, seeing how his harsh words had upset her, he put his arm round her narrow shoulders.

'Don't worry about it, Gran. We'll think of something else.'

But what, he wondered.

He went in search of Peter Barclay and together they made for the milking shed, where they could talk in private.

Colin explained what had happened.

'Gran says we must find another way to pay for all this,' he finished, gesturing towards the new milk-cooling unit. 'I don't think she realises how heavily we're committed, though I've tried to tell her.'

Though they talked it over for some time, neither could come up with a solution to Westgate's financial crisis. It would take some sort of miracle to make the place viable again.

Hazel had been very quiet over the past day or two and Susan eyed her anxiously as they sat together over coffee. She had noticed the girl was avoiding Peter Barclay and she wondered if anything had happened between them.

'I think I'll go home after all,' Hazel said suddenly.

Susan looked steadily at her. 'You aren't upset about anything, are you?' she asked.

The colour flew into Hazel's cheeks, but she avoided her sister's eyes.

Couldn't Susan see how Peter felt about her? Couldn't she see it in his eyes every time he looked at her?

'What could have upset me?' she asked sharply.

'I don't know,' Susan replied. 'It's just that you seem so down. Are you fed up here?'

'Of course not. I just want to go home for a day or two, that's all. I'll be able to collect the mail . . . '

And it would give her time to come to terms with herself and her feelings, she thought.

Susan rose and gave her an affectionate hug.

'Well, don't stay away too long. I like having you here,' she confessed.

★   ★   ★

Hazel travelled back to Netherdale the following day. The house felt cold and musty, and she went round opening all the windows and lit the fire. How quiet it seemed without her father, who was still away on business.

She made herself something to eat, then had just sat down to relax and was thinking she'd ring Tony to catch up on the news, when the doorbell rang.

She opened the door to find Laurence McKnight on the step.

'Uncle Laurie!' she cried with pleasure. 'Come in.'

'I saw the smoke signals,' he said, indicating the fire. 'You're home, then.'

'Only for a couple of days,' she said. 'Dad's still away.'

'I know. I suppose he's told you about that fish farm in Kilgordon? I thought it would be a fine undertaking for the two of us.'

'I know! Susan and I both think it'd be great for him. It'd be much better for his health, too — he's under way too much pressure at Carmichael's.'

'Right.' Laurence nodded in agreement. 'The problem is, although I thought we had plenty of time to decide and make plans, we haven't. The people who are selling the fish farm need to know as soon as possible whether or not we're going to buy it. So I'll have to get in touch with your dad.'

'I'll give you his phone number,' Hazel told him, reaching for a pen and paper.

'He'll have to make up his mind quickly. But — you know he'll likely have to put the house up for sale if he decides to come in with me?' he asked her.

Hazel's thoughts were in a whirl. She had realised that there would be changes, but they had seemed too far in the future for any immediate concern — until now. What was she going to do? She would lose the only home she had ever known.

'I'll ring your dad tomorrow,' Uncle Laurie was saying. 'When are you going back to Westgate?'

'The day after tomorrow, probably,' Hazel replied.

'That's good. You shouldn't be here on your own.'

Next morning, Hazel phoned Tony at

work and invited him for supper, then spent the rest of the day cleaning and tidying the house and planning their meal. She was looking forward to trying some interesting recipes as a change from the wholesome farmhouse food she'd been eating at Westgate.

When Tony arrived, he swept her into his arms and kissed her soundly.

'It isn't fair of you to stay away for so long,' he declared.

She pushed him away, laughing.

'It's only been a week or two!'

'Well, it seems like years to me. Let me look at you. Have you got a milk-maid complexion?'

'I doubt it since I never became a milk-maid.'

'A goose-girl, then. More importantly, how many paintings have you finished?' he asked.

'None, yet,' Hazel replied, guiltily realising she hadn't given a thought to painting — yet once it had seemed the most important thing in her life.

Tony was as bright as ever, but he

seemed young and boyish in comparison with Peter.

Peter — she couldn't shake his dark face from her thoughts, and listened with only half an ear while Tony told her his latest news.

'This chap I know wants a painting of his dog,' he was saying, 'but I'm really busy working for an exhibition and I can't spare the time. How are you fixed? Hazel? Hazel?'

'What? Oh, sorry, I was miles away, thinking about . . .'

'About what?' His eyes narrowed a little. 'Or should I say who? Peter Barclay perhaps? I had noticed he was creeping into more and more of your letters.'

A blush crept up her cheeks, but she looked away with annoyance.

'He's only the farm manager at Westgate,' she said. 'He — he doesn't pay any attention to me.'

Tony looked closely at her. He knew her so well, and something in her voice alerted him to the fact that Peter

Barclay had made quite an impression on her.

'You haven't gone and fallen for him, have you?' he asked.

'Of course not!' she cried. 'Anyway, I think he cares for someone else,' she whispered.

'And you mind about that?'

She looked at him miserably, then slowly nodded.

'I can't help it, Tony. He's like no-one I've ever known. I can't help being a little attracted to him.'

'Don't go falling for him, Hazel,' Tony warned. 'He doesn't sound right for you — you need someone like me.' He grinned.

'Oh, Tony.' She tried to smile through a mist of tears.

His eyes were serious as they rested on her. He didn't want her to fall in love with anyone else. They had always been good friends, but he knew that his feelings went deeper than that. He loved Hazel . . . though now wasn't the time to tell her.

'What about this dog, then?' Hazel asked, blowing her nose. 'Is it going to sit for me?' she managed to joke.

'As if! You'd work from a photograph.'

'Right . . .' she said thoughtfully, and he assumed she was thinking about whether or not to take on the project, so he was surprised by her next words.

'I'm thinking of looking for my own flat. Dad would be selling this house if he went to Kilgordon so I'd have to find something then anyway.'

Insecurity gnawed at her. Perhaps soon she'd have no real home.

She knew Susan would probably want her to go to Westgate, but she couldn't bear to watch Peter's eyes following her sister everywhere.

'Don't forget you can move in with me,' Tony offered. 'We — we could make it legit, if you like,' he added lightly.

'You're a dear friend, Tony,' she said and he pulled her close and kissed her. He knew he still hadn't won her love.

★ ★ ★

Leila Sutherland put down the phone with a smile of satisfaction. Colin would be with them for lunch the following day, stopping off on his way home from a trip to Edinburgh.

'Can you make a point of being here for lunch tomorrow?' she asked Daniel as she went to join him in the sitting-room.

He looked up from his crossword puzzle and smiled a little.

'You're the one who's usually out to lunch, dear,' he said. 'Of course I'll be here.'

'You disappear pretty frequently yourself these days,' she countered, 'with all the new projects you've taken on since you retired.'

'They don't take me to London, though, do they?'

'I wonder why Colin is going to Edinburgh,' mused Leila, ignoring her husband's pointed remark . . .

Daniel flicked back a lock of his

lengthening hair. He was wearing one of the new shirts he had bought with such pride, and although few people would have given his appearance a second glance, Leila looked at him rather unhappily.

She had the feeling that he was trying hard to update his image to please her, and there was an odd little ache in her heart as she looked at him.

How could she tell him that there was no need for him to change? He really looked better in well-made casual clothes like his old sweater and trousers, she thought.

Daniel made a special effort the following morning, and he was waiting for Colin when he arrived at lunch-time. Surprise at his father's new image showed plainly in Colin's eyes, but his mother hurried forward and squeezed his arm warningly as she kissed his cheek.

Despite the constant arguments over his career, there was a great love between Colin and his parents.

'I've made your favourite — chicken casserole,' Leila told him. 'Why were you in Edinburgh, anyway?' she asked casually.

'I was taking some oil paintings to be valued. I found them in the attic at Westgate. I don't suppose it's any secret that we need fresh capital badly, and Gran refuses to mortgage the land.'

'I could have told you that.' Leila said rather heavily.

'Well, anyway, she wants me to find another way to get the money, so I'm having the pictures valued. I doubt if they're Rembrandts or Renoirs, but you never know.'

Daniel was looking at his son anxiously, remembering how he and Leila had been helped by her parents when they'd bought their house. How much did Colin need? He would make the opportunity to have a word with him in private, he decided.

They enjoyed a pleasant family lunch, without arguments, and coffee in the lounge afterwards. Draining her cup, Leila glanced at the time and excused herself.

'My turn for Oxfam this afternoon,' she said. 'I couldn't get anyone to change with me. I don't suppose you can stay the night, Colin?'

'I'm afraid not. I've got to get back to help Peter.'

'Try to arrange a weekend soon, then, and bring Susan. It'll be a break for her.'

After Leila had gone, Daniel lost no time in talking to his son.

'How much do you need?' he asked. 'Can't we help? If it isn't too big a sum, I can talk to your mother. I've got a reasonably good pension and . . . '

'Oh, Dad, that's just what I'd expect you to say, but we're talking in five figures at least. I'm committed to a whole new milk-cooling plant and buildings to accommodate it. And I need more stock, too.'

'Your grandfather wasn't slow to help us,' Daniel observed.

'I know, but it was different then.'

Colin bit his lip. How could he tell him that it was Mr Campbell's generosity that had started the downfall of Westgate?

'You're looking very smart these days, Dad,' Colin commented to change tack. 'What happened to that ancient Harris tweed jacket? It suited you.'

'I was a sloppy mess! I've got to keep up with your mother, you know. She's still young and beautiful . . . and very attractive to other men. She doesn't want an old fogey for a husband.'

He laughed and Colin joined in, but nevertheless, the words stayed in Colin's mind as he drove home.

His father had spoken lightly, but hadn't there been a ring of truth, even a hint of anxiety, in his voice?

He recalled how smart and, yes, youthful his mother had looked as she prepared to go out and felt vaguely uneasy. Surely nothing could go wrong with his parents' marriage after all these years — could it?

* ★ ★

Gradually Susan had been settling down into Westgate and accepting the old farmhouse as her home, and she had got it looking as bright and pretty as she could without spending a penny extra. Mrs Campbell had helped a lot by rekindling one of her old interests, that of making colourful rag rugs.

'It's fine to be keeping my hands busy,' she told Susan, 'even if I have to sit about such a lot. I learned how to make rugs from my mother, but when I got married, there was never any time.

'I was even busier than you, lass, for it was oil lamps and cooking on the kitchen range in those days. You'll not believe it, but that stove you grumble about was a great boon to me when I got it!'

'Oh, I can believe it, but it's had its day I'm afraid, Mrs Campbell,' Susan said.

'You're doing fine with it, lass. Your scones are a lot lighter these days. Now, help me to cut up these cloths, and I'll get on with a few more rugs.'

When Hazel arrived back, she was only too happy to help with the rugs, too, especially since it kept her in the kitchen or sitting room, well out of the way of any risk of running into Peter Barclay.

However, after Colin left for Edinburgh, she pulled on her gumboots and ventured outdoors to lend a hand, while Susan went wearily to deal with the hens. Normally Hazel helped her, but Susan had assured her that she could manage very well on her own for once.

When Peter finished cleaning out the byre with Hazel's help, he walked over to the hen-house to lend Susan a hand. The sight of her tired face caught at his heart.

'Here, let me help,' he said roughly.

His eyes devoured her face, and he had to exercise all his willpower to stop himself from gathering her into his arms and kissing her passionately, and promising to look after her for ever.

He loved Susan so much that the longing was a constant ache in his heart. He knew he should leave the farm, but he couldn't wrench himself away from her. The thought of perhaps never seeing her again was too painful.

Unaware of the turmoil raging inside him, Susan smiled and wearily tucked a stray curl hair back behind her ear.

'It's OK, I'm finished now,' she assured him as she turned to go back indoors.

Peter's eyes followed her, then he turned — to find Hazel standing beside him, her eyes blazing in her pale face as she stared at him

'You've fallen in love with her, haven't you?' she accused him in a low voice.

His face drained of colour.

'What — what do you mean?' he asked in a hoarse voice.

'You know very well. You're in love with her. But you're wasting your time. After all, she's only just married Colin and she adores him. She'll never turn to you,' she cried passionately.

'You . . . you're just being silly,' Peter muttered.

He felt suddenly exposed and vulnerable, and the girl's words rang painfully true.

'Oh, Peter, you're so wrong. You're special and . . . ' She moved forward, as if to stand against him.

'That's enough,' he told her roughly. 'You've said enough!'

They stared at one another and she saw that his face was full of pain, but she felt as if his suffering was only a reflection of her own.

For a moment there was silence, then, 'I'm going home,' he said. 'Susan asked me to supper, but make my apologies, will you? I've had enough for today.'

Hazel watched him walk away, fighting the tears that threatened. She loved him. She loved him deeply and passionately — and as hopelessly as he loved Susan.

Mrs Campbell had been dozing in

her chair by the window, but had stirred uneasily as their raised voices reached her ears. However, after the first few words she was wide awake, and frozen in amazement.

She had often thought that young Peter seemed too ready to give Susan a hand, and now she knew why.

She would have to think deeply before deciding what to do.

* * *

The rain-washed streets had never looked more beautiful to Leila Sutherland as she and Robert Chisholm drove to the station to catch the train for London.

Her smart luggage was well packed, with pride of place being given to a new midnight-blue velvet dress which would be perfect for a special occasion.

'I can hardly believe I'm going to London with you.' She sighed as she settled into her seat beside him. 'It should be such an exciting conference, too.'

'Yes.' Then he grinned and squeezed her fingers. 'Though nothing compares to the excitement of sitting here like this with you. Are you happy to see me?'

'Oh, Robert, I know it's wrong,' she said, 'but yes, I'm terribly happy to be with you again.'

He put his arm round her shoulders and drew her close.

'My darling . . . '

'Robert, don't,' she whispered. 'Some-one might see us. Oh, it's so awful having to look over one's shoulder all the time. It makes it all rather sordid, somehow.'

'Do you think so? To me it just makes it all the more exciting!' he teased. 'Seriously, my sweet, I only know I'm happy for the first time in weeks.'

'Me, too,' she confessed.

A sudden vision of Daniel waving her off from the house, his bright shirt and rather untidy hair looking slightly incongruous, caught at her heart, but the memory dissolved as she looked up into Robert's eyes.

She had no power to resist the attraction he aroused in her. When she was with him, Daniel belonged to another world, a world that ceased to matter.

Already the excitement of everything that lay ahead was absorbing her, and Robert Chisholm shared in and was a part of all that excitement.

Life could be so wonderful. Why worry about the future when the present was all she desired?

The conference was the liveliest she had ever attended and she was pleased to hear how well received Robert's speech was. They wcrc both bubbling with happiness when they met in the bar afterwards, and later, when she had bathed and changed into her velvet gown for dinner, she stood for a long time gazing at her reflection in the mirror. Her eyes were sparkling, a flush of anticipation made her complexion glow . . . and she knew she had never looked more beautiful.

Robert's eyes said it all when they met to go in to dinner.

'I thought I was hungry, but one look at you is food for the gods,' he said.

'You'll soon get your appetite back.' She laughed dismissively. 'I just love being in London again. It suits me. There's such a wonderful atmosphere here.'

'You bring it with you,' he told her. 'You're so beautiful, I can hardly believe you're real,' he flattered her.

After a delicious meal over which he flirted and teased her, they took to the dance floor, circling slowly, cheek to cheek.

'You're like thistledown,' he murmured in her ear, tightening his arms around her, and she nestled closer to him, her senses singing.

'I'm having a wonderful time,' she told him as the music ended and they returned to their table.

She was aware that they made a very striking couple who drew the attention of those around them, and she allowed her eyes to sweep over the crowded room with delight. But suddenly she saw a tall young man rising from one of the tables and her smile froze — he reminded her of Colin.

Robert sensed the change in her.

'What is it?' he asked softly. 'Can't you forget about everything but us?'

'I . . . yes . . . at least, I thought I could, but — ' She saw his eyes darken. 'It's just that I saw someone who reminded me of my son.' She mentally shook herself and forced a smile. 'Forget it. I won't spoil this wonderful evening, I promise.'

'It's too precious to spoil,' he told her.

★ ★ ★

They danced the night away, teasing and laughing and enjoying the magic of what they had found together, but eventually midnight drew near and, like Cinderella, she knew it was almost over.

The music ended, and they were

both very quiet as Robert saw her to her room. As she took the key out of her bag, Robert's hand closed over it and he inserted it into the lock.

'No, Robert,' she whispered, as he made to enter the room. 'No, this is where we draw the line. We mustn't let ourselves — or anybody else — down.'

'Is that truly what you want?' he asked, and he took her in his arms and kissed her until her senses swam.

Her heart was racing as though it would burst but she managed to smile shakily.

'It's what I want,' she said breathlessly. 'I want you to go now.'

Without another word, he turned and left her, and she closed the door behind him, feeling emotionally drained.

It was all over. Her night of enchantment had ended.

Sadly she removed her gown and put on her ivory silk nightdress and matching robe, then sat down at the dressing-table to brush out her hair, sighing at her reflection, seeing the light in her eyes die.

Tomorrow everything would be over; she'd be back in Netherdale — back with Daniel.

There was a light tap at her door and her heart leapt. Robert?

Her knees trembled as she rose and went to open the door.

Robert stood staring at her, his eyes brilliant in the soft glow from the room. Without a word he stepped forward and took her gently in his arms.

'Leila,' he whispered, 'I had to come back. Please don't send me away.'

For a moment reality shone bright in her mind — the need to remain loyal to Daniel, the need to find help for Colin, and the need to — to —

But then everything was blotted out as Robert kissed her again and again and their passion spun a web of enchantment around her, gossamer threads, light as thistledown, but irresistibly binding her into a dreamlike state of unreality.

This time she had no power to send him away . . .

Regrets . . .

There was little time to dwell on the previous night as Leila and Robert rushed to have breakfast, get packed and grab a taxi in time to catch their train.

Waking in the cold light of day, Leila had been appalled by what had happened, but Robert openly expressed his happiness, obviously in no way touched by remorse. Leila knew they'd have to talk.

The train wasn't busy and there was no one close to their reserved seats, offering them privacy and seclusion. Robert quickly took her in his arms and kissed her lovingly.

'I'm so happy, my darling,' he said. 'You must know now that we belong together, you and I. Last night proved that. I'm so much in love with you.'

'No, Robert, please.' She struggled

free of his embrace. 'You're going much too fast for me. We must talk. Last night was — well, a sort of enchantment. We got carried away . . . it was such an exciting response to your speech . . . then the lovely meal, the dancing . . . But now we must come down to earth.'

'But that doesn't mean we can forget everything. We've gone too far for that,' he protested.

'Yes, you're right about that — we have gone too far. Have you thought about what this could do to your career if it came out? You've not even been elected yet. Such a scandal would finish any chance you might have!'

'I'd give it all up for you, Leila. If you'll divorce Daniel, I'll happily sacrifice my career for you.'

'But I — I can't leave Daniel, Robert. I still love him. We've loved each other for all these years, and I can't stop loving him because I feel something for you.'

She was struggling to put her feelings

into words because she barely understood them herself. There was one feeling, however, that she did recognise completely and that was remorse. How could she have done this to Daniel?

Robert was shaking his head.

'Oh, my darling, you're too young and vital for him. He's retired, for goodness sake! Whereas you and I — oh, we could have such a wonderful life together!' His eyes were shining in his enthusiasm and her heart leapt irrationally at the thought.

Robert was so good to be with — such fun and so exciting. But she knew that Daniel's kindly face would never be far from her thoughts. He was so familiar to her, and very, very dear.

How could she love two men at the same time? But that's how it felt — her heart seemed to be split in two.

Suddenly she thought of Colin. How hurt he would be if he found out how she had let his father down.

She fought back tears of shame.

'I have to think of my family, Robert,'

she said. 'Besides Daniel, there are Colin and Susan, and my mother. You don't have a family so you can't understand what this would do to them.'

'But I'd give up everything for you,' he told her.

'Yes, I know — and in doing it you'd be letting too many people down.'

Leila stared disconsolately out of the far window for a few moments and he watched her, hardly daring to speak yet desperate to persuade her, wondering if he was really losing her.

'Didn't you say you wanted to ask me something about Colin?' he said after a while, in an effort to ease the tension between them.

'What?' She roused herself from the unhappy depths of her thoughts. 'Oh, that . . .' How could she ask a favour of him now?

But it was for Colin, her son, and perhaps in some small way it would atone for her betrayal of her family.

'I just wondered if you know if Colin

would be eligible for an EC grant? I told you about his circumstances.'

'I'll try to find out about it.' He took her hand. 'Let me think about it,' he told her, feeling the tension between them relax as they got on to this safer, impersonal subject. 'I'd have to know all the details but you can tell me all that next Tuesday. There's to be a committee meeting then . . . '

Leila bit her lip. She had been thinking how unwise it would be to see him again.

'We've got to keep seeing each other,' he said, as if he had read her thoughts.

'I — I don't know,' she whispered.

'We must see each other,' he persisted. 'It's the only way we can decide what we're going to do. Besides, how can I solve any problems for Colin if we can't talk them over?'

She knew he was right, just as she knew she had to try to resist this overwhelming attraction she felt for him. Deep down she didn't feel very proud of herself, for more than one reason. Was she really going to stoop so low as to let herself use Colin, her only son, as her excuse for keeping in touch with her lover?

Robert ran her home from the station in silence.

'Until Tuesday, then,' he said as he dropped her outside her house, and the air crackled with the unspoken emotions raging between them.

★   ★   ★

Colin drove home in a happier frame of mind after the break in Edinburgh and Netherdale, but as he neared Westgate the problems that lay ahead began to intrude once again.

How long would the bank manager be prepared to wait before insisting on repayment of the advance on that loan?

Susan rushed out to meet him almost the instant he stepped from the car.

'Oh, Colin, I'm so glad to see you,' she cried almost tearfully, flinging her arms around his neck. 'It's been so long!'

'Only two days,' he said, laughing a little as he kissed her.

'It seemed like years,' she said, and his face grew more sober as he walked indoors with her.

She seemed almost desperate to see him again. Was it so bad for her here without him?

He knew she'd found it very difficult at first but he'd thought she was beginning to settle down. Now, suddenly, he wasn't so sure, and the knowledge struck at his heart, adding to the heaviness which was already settling on him again.

Colin didn't have time to brood on it for long, though, as the following morning he was up even earlier than normal to catch up on his usual routine.

Peter was unusually quiet, Colin noticed, as they worked together, and he hoped nothing was amiss.

Eventually, he grinned at the other man.

'You're not saying much today,' he said. 'What's wrong? No faults to find?' he teased.

'What could be wrong?' Peter asked defensively.

'I'm sure I don't know, but anyone would think you were in love, the way you've been mooning about.'

Colin was grinning broadly, but the smile faded as he looked Peter full in the face and saw his stunned expression.

'Don't tell me I've hit the nail on the head!' he exclaimed. '*Is* there a girl? Who is she?'

Peter looked stricken as he stared back at Colin, his eyes full of distress and guilt, and Colin's face hardened as a vague suspicion began to form in his mind.

'Who is it?' he demanded more harshly.

Hazel had come into the barn just in time to overhear the conversation and her first instinct was to protect Susan.

She stepped forward, smiling brightly.

'Oh, so you've guessed, have you?' she said to Colin, her cheeks reddening. Then she turned to take Peter's arm and grasped it tightly. 'It's me, of course. Who else?'

As relief swept through Colin, he didn't see the look of anger which Peter cast in Hazel's direction.

How dare she say such a thing! But her eyes challenged him to keep quiet, and he bent his head as though in silent acknowledgment.

'It's nothing serious at the moment,' Hazel added swiftly. 'We're not engaged or anything like that.'

'So congratulations aren't in order yet? Oh, well, I'd better leave you two lovebirds to it. Do excuse me!' He grinned mischievously, then turned to walk indoors.

Peter turned on Hazel as soon as he judged that Colin would be out of earshot.

'How could you say such a thing?' he raged. 'You know there's nothing between us — and never will be,' he added.

'I know that. But I also know how you feel about Susan, and I don't want Colin to know, too. Can't you see how he would react? Susan would get hurt. And you don't want that, do you?'

Colin had gone straight indoors to see what Susan had to say about her sister's romance.

She looked at him in amazement.

'They're what? It's news to me!' she said, frowning.

'Oh. Well, maybe Hazel just hasn't had time to tell you yet. Aren't you pleased? Peter's a good lad . . . '

'Pleased to hear my sister has fallen in love with a — a farm-hand?' she cried, then bit her lip when she saw Colin's face which had suddenly gone white.

'*You* married a farm-hand!' he said angrily.

'I know.' She turned away, trying to control her tears as he stormed out of the house without giving her the chance to try to explain. Oh, what a mess! she thought.

A little while later, when she could hear Hazel pottering about in her room, she decided she really had to talk to the girl about this and went upstairs.

She hesitated at the door for a moment — she hated to seem to be interfering — but this was too important to leave. She couldn't let her young sister ruin her life without trying to do something to prevent it.

So, taking a deep breath, she tapped lightly on the door and went in.

'Colin told me about you and Peter,' she began without preamble. Then, 'I don't want you to marry him — he's a farmer,' she said bluntly.

As Hazel looked at her askance, she went on, 'Yes, I know *I* did, but it's hard work if you aren't born to it. Believe me, I know!'

Hazel shrugged nonchalantly. 'I've seen for myself how much has to be done. I think I can be the best judge of whether or not I'm prepared for it'

'Well, all I'm saying is — don't encourage Peter, that's all. I think you'd be making a huge mistake,' Susan advised.

What did she mean, Hazel wondered. What was so wrong with farming?

Seeing her puzzlement, Susan went on to explain.

'I just want you to have a better life. You're an artist, with a wonderful talent,' she said. 'You shouldn't let it go to waste. By all means, have a fling with Peter if you like him that much. Just don't get committed,' she added as she rose to leave the room. 'You've plenty of time before you should think about settling down.'

Neither girl mentioned the discussion when Hazel came down later, but the atmosphere between them remained slightly more strained than usual.

They were busy in the kitchen silently preparing vegetables for supper when they heard a car drive into the yard, and a moment later were astonished when their father rapped at the door.

'Surprise! I've just finished in Glasgow and I'm heading home, but I thought I'd drive the extra miles and come to see you both,' he told them. 'Colin, too. I have a big decision to make and it concerns all of us.'

Susan enveloped him in a warm hug.

'It's lovely to see you, Dad,' she said, her throat thick with tears at the sight of him. She had missed him a great deal over the past few weeks.

Hazel, too, rushed to hug him, while Susan put the kettle on, then they all sat round the dining-table, sipping tea and munching biscuits, more cheerful than they had been for ages now that they were all together again.

Once they'd caught up on the gossip, Mr Ingrams broached the other reason for his visit.

'I only have a few days left before I have to give your Uncle Laurie my decision about this fish farm business. I'll admit I'm very tempted, but I just don't know what to do for the best. What do you two girls think?'

'I think you should go for it,' Susan

told him without hesitation. 'You know you'll love it.'

'I know, but it's not just as simple as that. There's the house,' he commented. 'I'd have to move up to Kilgordon, so it would mean selling the house — your home.'

He had turned to look at Hazel, whose heart had suddenly plunged to her shoes. But she rallied bravely. After all their father had done for them over the years, this was the least she could do for him in return.

'Then sell the house, Daddy,' she said clearly. 'If you're worrying about me, don't. I'll soon sort myself out with someplace to stay, honestly.'

'You're sure?' he pressed, and when she nodded, he smiled, a wide smile of happiness they hadn't seen on his face for too long. It was all they needed to reassure them that they were doing the right thing.

He stood up. 'Right then — I'll phone Laurence and give him the go-ahead right now!'

Tony was delighted when Hazel paid him a surprise visit, and very pleased with the painting she had done of his client's dog.

'This is great,' he said. 'You've got over your slump, my angel, and you're painting like the good Lord intended!'

Hazel grinned, deeply pleased with his praise. Oh, it had been nice that her family had admired her work, but Tony was different. He knew what to look for in a painting, and he was so honest with her that she knew his praise was genuine.

'Have you missed me?' he asked, coming to take her in his arms.

She leaned against him for a moment. She knew Tony so well, and no-one could offer her more comfort than he.

'Oh, maybe a little,' she teased. 'But I'm only home for a short while,' she told him. 'The house is being sold up now that Dad's moving to Kilgordon so

I'll have to go back to the farm for now.'

'Why go back there?' he asked, then his eyes sharpened. 'It's Peter Barclay, isn't it?'

'In a way, but not quite what you think,' she returned. How could she explain that she felt she had to be there, beside Susan, to protect her from the temptation of Peter's love.

'I'm afraid, Hazel,' he said, showing a rare vulnerability. He was always so confident, so carefree. 'I'm scared that you'll fall in love with someone other than me when my back is turned.'

'I don't feel anything like that for anybody,' she said firmly, and he sighed, taking the point.

'Anyway,' he went on, resuming his usual bright manner, 'I've got some good news. Six of my paintings are to be included in an exhibition. If they sell, then I've got an agent wanting other work. It will be the jam on our bread, my sweet, and we can get married any time you like.'

Hazel looked into his eager face. He

always spoke in such a teasing way that she rarely took him seriously, but now she could see that he was deeply in earnest about wanting to marry her.

For a brief moment, she caught a glimpse of a future where she and Tony might very well be happy together. Then suddenly the feelings of confusion and bewilderment descended again.

'I'm sorry — I can't decide now, Tony,' she told him. 'I'm just so mixed up.'

'OK, but when you wake up one morning and realise that only I can help unravel all that confusion, remember — I'll be here.'

Somehow that was the most comforting thing she had heard all week.

Hazel returned to Westgate still feeling confused and she was happy to settle into the familiarity of the farmhouse routine and help Susan with the chores.

The telephone shrilled mid-morning. It was the art dealer for Colin and Hazel was sent to find him.

Susan slipped away and left him to talk privately, but after a short while he joined her in the kitchen. She could tell from his crestfallen face that it wasn't good news.

'Well, that's that,' he told her flatly. 'Those paintings I took to be valued? They may fetch a few hundred, but it's hardly enough to pay off all our debts.'

They were staring at each other in dismay when they heard the crunch of car wheels in the yard. Susan looked out of the window and her heart sank as she recognised the tall, well-dressed man getting out of the car and reaching for his briefcase.

'It's Mr Wilson, the bank manager,' she said.

She saw Colin's shoulders slump and defeat drift into his eyes.

'Well, I guess this is it,' he said. 'I'll take him into the study.'

The older man sat down heavily, almost as disappointed as Colin that things weren't going to plan. He snapped open his briefcase.

'I take it that Mrs Campbell is still unwilling to sign these papers as security for your loan?' he asked.

Colin nodded. 'You know my grandmother, Mr Wilson . . . '

'Then I'm afraid we'll have to negotiate new terms. The money advanced to you will require to be repaid in fairly large instalments, you understand, since we no longer have any security — and the first payment will be due at the end of the month.

'I'm sure you'll be in touch,' he said quietly. 'And — I'm sorry things have become so hard for you.'

Susan sought out Colin as soon as she heard the car leaving.

'What did he say?' she asked anxiously.

'What did you expect him to say?' His voice was so brusque and sharp that Susan drew back as though she had been slapped.

'I know this is hard for you, but it affects me, too!' she cried.

'You know nothing about it!' he

snapped. 'Your job is to . . . '

'Run your home . . . *our* home. But how many other things besides? Or doesn't that count?'

'Oh, don't you start!' he shouted and rushed out of the door, banging it behind him.

Miserably Susan stared at the door, forcing back the tears, a hard lump of bitterness and resentment rising in her throat.

★ ★ ★

Leila Sutherland had been very subdued since her return from London. The sheer horror and guilt of her behaviour with Robert lay heavily on her heart.

When Robert rang for the first time since they'd got back, there was panic in her voice as she answered the phone.

'I'll call in and see you this afternoon,' he told her.

'No, Robert, please, you mustn't! We mustn't see each other again. I — I feel awful.'

'But I have to see you, my dear. I've been very busy on your behalf, or rather, on Colin's. Look, I've managed to arrange something for him. Is Daniel out as usual this afternoon?'

'Yes . . . no! No, don't come here.'

'I think I'd better. I think we need to talk, my darling,' and he ended the call before she could protest any more.

Leila's eyes were red and swollen from crying when she opened the door to Robert that afternoon, but he walked in briskly and as soon as the door was closed, he pulled her into his arms and tried to kiss her.

Leila pushed him away.

'It's no use, Robert. I just can't behave like this. I must have been mad — and you, too. We mustn't ever, ever be alone again.'

'But, Leila . . . '

'No, it's no use. I can't break up my marriage.'

He stared at her, then gently guided her into a chair, his expression bleak. He loved her passionately, and he was sure that she loved him, too. However, now he could see that her basic honesty and integrity had triumphed.

'At least let me help Colin,' he suggested. 'I can arrange a loan for him at a very favourable rate of interest.'

For just a second she was tempted, but then, realising the dangers, she slowly shook her head.

'I don't want to involve Colin, Robert. I shouldn't have asked, though I — I'm deeply grateful.'

'I see.' He sighed deeply, all his pain and bewilderment all too evident in the weary sound. 'I'll go now,' he said quietly, 'but I can't promise never to see you again . . . '

★   ★   ★

'That was Tony,' Hazel said as she put down the phone and returned to the kitchen where she was helping Susan wash the floors and windows.

Susan's heart seemed to be permanently heavy these days, but she forced a bright smile for Hazel's benefit.

'He's found a flat for me,' Hazel went on. 'The one on the floor below his own is coming vacant. And since the garage says I can work there full time if I want, I could afford it. So I think I'll take a look at it.'

'Well, don't go signing anything until Daddy takes a look at it,' Susan warned her, then continued, 'I told you that you could stay here, remember,' but her voice lacked conviction.

The atmosphere at the farm wasn't easy at the moment. Susan and Colin were inclined to be quiet and offhand with one another, and Hazel had wondered if she was in the way.

A few days later, with Hazel in Netherdale to look at the flat, Susan felt even more miserable. Colin was upstairs changing, ready to keep an appointment with the bank at Westport, while she was frantically slicing up tinned ham to make a sandwich for lunch.

When he appeared in the kitchen he

peered over her shoulder.

'What's that?' he asked suspiciously.

'Ham for sandwiches. I'll make you a pot of tea.'

'But I thought you were making stew,' Colin protested. 'For heavens sake, Susan — I've been working since seven. I need more than a sandwich to keep me going. I'm starving!'

'I know, but the stew isn't ready yet,' Susan explained sulkily. 'And don't blame me. I put it on in plenty of time, but — it's that monster of a stove. It just sits there doing nothing. It's useless!'

'Did you clean out the flues? Remember I told you that they should be cleaned out once a week? You just don't try, Susan.'

Rage and frustration bubbled up in her. That Colin should say that when she was working her fingers to the bone! Well, finally she'd had enough.

'How dare you say that, Colin Sutherland!'

And she slammed out of the back

door, hardly knowing where she was going, but her steps taking her instinctively towards the barn.

His insult was ringing in her ears, and as she heard his car roar out of the yard, she let herself go in a storm of weeping.

★   ★   ★

'Why . . . Susan! What's wrong?' Suddenly Peter was beside her and her sobs only increased as he gathered her into his arms.

'Oh, Susan,' he whispered, 'Susan, I can't bear to see you so upset! I love you so much — I'd give anything in the world to make things easier for you.'

'Oh, Peter . . . '

She tried to free herself, but he was holding her very tightly, and after a moment she could feel the warmth and comfort of staying in his arms.

Colin had rejected her. It was a wife who could work like a farm-hand

and a skivvy that he wanted, not a wife who would adore him and cherish him, laugh with him and love him.

'I've loved you from the first moment I saw you,' Peter was saying. 'You must have known — you must have seen how I feel. Hazel knew. She understood that I'll never love anyone else.'

His lips were on hers, tender and questioning, and warmth seemed to fill her heart. Her arms crept round his neck . . .

'I've never known anyone like you,' Peter was murmuring into her hair, kissing her neck, setting her senses on fire.

She struggled against him. 'No, Peter,' she said faintly, stopping his caresses. 'No, this is wrong!'

'But I've wanted you for so long,' he told her. 'I've waited and watched and looked after you when I could. You know I have. I've tried to help you every way I can.

'I only stay here because of you. I've

longed for the moment when I could love you like this, waiting for you to turn to me. And I do love you — so much . . . '

It would be so easy to give in, to let herself forget everything but the fact that she was so greatly loved, but even as his lips closed on her own, she was pushing him away.

'No, Peter, no. It's no use. I — I'm Colin's wife. We mustn't . . . I shouldn't even have let you kiss me,' she told him, her chest heaving with agitation as she backed away 'I've let myself down, and — and Colin — and you! I — I don't know what got into me.'

And with that she was running again, out of the barn and back to the house. Was she to spend the rest of her life running from heartache, she wondered bleakly.

She found Mrs Campbell in the kitchen, wrapped in one of her old aprons, which was now black with soot, as were her arms, up to the elbows.

'I've got most of it out for you, lass,'

she said. 'I've brought down most of the soot.'

'Oh,' Susan sighed, her eyes again filling with tears, 'that was my job. You shouldn't be doing this.'

'We all do things we shouldn't at times,' the woman said, and eyed her shrewdly. 'But maybe there's no lasting damage done to either of us,' she murmured, then went on, 'You're a good lass, Susan.' The old woman nodded. 'Don't forget that Colin loves you.'

'He used to, maybe,' Susan said sadly. 'To be honest, I don't know how he feels any more.'

★ ★ ★

Peter handed in his notice to Colin a few days later.

'You'll soon get a student to help,' Peter told him. 'It'll do some good lad a favour. I'll leave the cottage ready for the next tenant.'

'But I thought you had something

245

going with Hazel,' Colin protested.

This resignation was a bolt from the blue to him. However, he had sensed a tension in Peter over these last few days, and wondered now if it was a lovers' tiff.

Peter's answer confirmed his suspicions.

'Oh, that was just a young girl's fancy,' he said, avoiding the other man's gaze. 'She soon got over that.'

Of course, the truth was that it wasn't Hazel he was running from, but Susan. He had to get away from Westgate, away from this love that had to be denied.

'I hope you'll keep in touch,' Colin said, completely unaware of the truth of the matter.

'We'll see,' Peter said non-committally. 'Look, if you like, I could — um — stay till the student arrives, and put him in the picture. OK?'

'OK,' Colin agreed.

Peter wasn't the only one who wanted to escape. Susan, too, wanted to get away. It seemed to her that a great barrier had dropped between her and Colin so that they just couldn't talk to one another.

'I've decided to go home for two days,' she told him later. 'But I've arranged for a lady from the village to come in, so you should manage all right.'

'Whatever. If you think running away from a bit of hard work will make you feel better, just you carry on,' he retorted bitterly, and she sighed in despair.

'I wish I could make you understand why I'm going, Colin. Our problem isn't the work, or the lack of money, and until you see that, we just can't talk to one another.'

She needed his love, she thought inwardly. She could accept anything, if only he'd show his love and appreciation for her, and while he seemed unable or unwilling to realise that, then they were no longer in harmony with one another.

'I'll visit your mum while I'm in Netherdale,' she told him. 'I'll only stay two days,' she offered, hoping that he would ask her not to go, to stay because he couldn't manage without her, because he needed her . . . But —

'Stay as long as you like,' he said roughly.

Truth Will Out

And so Susan went home to Netherdale, where she tried to throw off her
worries over the next two days.

Her father had signed the papers for
the purchase of the fish farm, there was
a large notice in the garden offering the
house for sale, and Susan was kept busy
helping him tie up all the loose ends.

Even so, she was determined to go to
see Colin's mother one afternoon,
though when she rang in the morning,
it was Daniel who answered the
telephone.

'Susan! Lovely to hear from you!
Leila? Yes, I'm sure she'd be delighted if
you dropped in this afternoon. She's
out shopping at the moment, then she's
having lunch with one of her committee
ladies, but she'll be free after that
— about two-thirty?

'Good, good — I'll leave her a

message to expect you about three. Sorry I'll miss you, but I'm just off out for the rest of the day myself. You take care now, m'dear.'

As it happened, Leila was late home, and she didn't notice the note Daniel had left propped up for her as she dropped her shopping on to the hall table.

As she caught sight of herself in the hall mirror, she realised she was losing weight. Her face had become pale and gaunt, and she was beginning to look every day of her years.

But it was guilt, not longing for Robert, that was eating into her soul, as the memory of that night in London came back to haunt her again and again.

If only Daniel wouldn't try so hard to cheer her up, she thought wretchedly, but his eyes were so full of kindness and innocence each time they looked into her own, that she felt as though he could read the guilt in hers and couldn't face him squarely.

The memory of the unhappiness she had caused Robert continued to torture her, too, and she felt tears of wretchedness begin to rise up and choke her again.

She stumbled blindly into the living room and sank onto the sofa, where she buried her face in her hands and gave way to a storm of weeping, as she had so many times recently when she had the house to herself.

She didn't hear Susan's gentle knock at the door and it was only when the girl was standing at the door of the living room that she realised she wasn't alone.

'Mrs Sutherland!' Susan cried. 'What's happened?'

Fear squeezed at Susan's heart. Was it Colin? She rushed over and knelt down beside the other woman.

'Please . . . Is it Colin? You've got to tell me,' she said. 'What's happened?'

Leila stared blindly at Susan, the tears glistening on her cheeks, and Susan was shocked by her appearance.

She had always admired the woman's beauty and elegance, but now Leila looked gaunt and thin, her eyes red and swollen with weeping.

'Are you ill?' Susan asked gently. 'Can't you tell me?'

Leila heaved a shuddering sigh and blew her nose, trying to regain a fraction of her usual composure.

'Oh, Susan, I did a terrible thing and I — I can't live with it. I just can't.' She turned her tormented eyes on the girl. 'Every time Daniel looks at me, I feel soiled inside.'

'What's happened?' Susan coaxed gently. 'It might help you to talk about it.'

'It — it was Robert Chisholm,' she admitted. 'In London. We stayed at the same hotel and . . . well, I don't have to spell it out. I didn't feel ready to accept old age when Daniel retired, and Robert offered fun and glamour . . .

'I know it was wrong, but I didn't realise just how much I would suffer for it.'

Susan's eyes were wide with shock. Then, unbidden, her thoughts swept to Peter Barclay. It would have been so easy to be swept off her feet. She had been feeling unloved, unwanted, taken for granted . . . she could understand how Leila felt.

'Is it over between you and Robert?' she asked.

'Yes! Yes, of course. I couldn't go on. But I feel so guilty. It's ruined my life.'

'Tell Daniel,' Susan said decisively. 'He'll understand. He loves you very much. And he'll accept it because he loves you. Only then will you be able to put it all behind you.'

She spoke with such quiet certainty that Leila felt herself believing it and growing calm, and wondered at the self-assurance and wisdom of her young daughter-in-law.

Susan made her a cup of coffee and sat with her for a bit, but the girl had been gone for over an hour before Daniel came home.

He couldn't fail to notice her eyes,

still red and swollen from weeping, and as she she stared at him nervously he echoed Susan's questions.

'What is it? What's happened?'

She drew a deep breath.

'Daniel, I have to talk to you.'

His heart lurched at the tone of her voice.

'What is it?'

'It — it's about Robert Chisholm. Something happened between us — in London.' She bent her head to avoid his gaze, unable to bear what she knew she would see there. 'But it's over now, Daniel. I swear it's all over.'

'How far did it go?' he asked harshly, grasping her shoulders, forcing her to look at him. 'Leila?'

'I . . . we . . . ' she stammered, and he snorted in disgust.

'It's all right, you don't have to spell it out for me.'

She clutched at his sleeve.

'It only happened once, I swear, Daniel. I — I put a stop to it. We're not going to see one another again, I promise. Oh, Daniel, I've been feeling so terrible, so guilty. But Susan made me realise that I had to tell you — '

'Susan? So she knows, too?'

He thrust her away from him and turned his back on her.

'She's the only one who knows,' she whispered. 'She's a sweet girl. She won't tell Colin, and no one else will ever know. Oh, Daniel, can you ever forgive me?'

The words were uttered with such pain that he turned and her tear-filled eyes met his. But as she stretched out her hand in mute appeal, he pulled away.

'Give me time, Leila, please — just give me time . . . '

★ ★ ★

Mrs Campbell sat at the window, watching Colin's tall figure stride across the farmyard. She had decided that while Susan was in Netherdale, she would have a talk with him, make him understand the pressure the girl was under, trying to cope with being a newly-wed and with life on the farm. She had noticed with dismay how short he was with Susan these days and was disappointed that he was being so insensitive.

She called him as he entered the kitchen.

'I was wanting a wee word with you — about you and Susan. You're awfully hard on the lass when anyone can see she's trying her best. And it troubles me to see the way you're at odds with one another.'

Colin's face hardened.

'It's better if we don't talk about Susan, Gran.'

'You've got to go easier on her, Colin. Now that Peter has gone, this is a fine opportunity for you both to start afresh.'

'Start afresh? Now that Peter has gone? What are you talking about, Gran?' He stared at her suspiciously and too late she realised she'd said the wrong thing as he smacked his forehead in realisation.

'Oh, I see! Well, I've been the blind fool, haven't I? I could see a mile away that Peter Barclay was in love, but I was stupid enough to think it was Hazel. But it wasn't, was it? It was Susan! It's been going on under my nose the whole time, hasn't it?'

'Colin, no!' Mrs Campbell cried, deeply upset. 'You've got it wrong, lad. Oh, maybe Peter did take a fancy to Susan, but she didn't encourage him.'

'I don't believe it!' he shouted, beside himself with anger and jealousy.

Mrs Campbell shook her head.

'You're making a big mistake, lad,' she told him, and was left sighing deeply as he stormed away. When he had calmed down, she had no doubt he would see how stupidly he was behaving, but at the moment he wasn't going to listen to reason.

Colin was busy out in one of the yards when Susan eventually arrived home, but Mrs Campbell was sitting in her favourite chair in the living room.

'I'm glad to see you back, lass,' she said, but her hand shook as Susan came to kiss her and it crossed Susan's mind that the woman didn't look well. She hoped she hadn't been overdoing things while she'd been away.

Susan didn't have a chance to talk to Colin until they were in their bedroom that night. She chatted eagerly for a while, then noticed how subdued he was.

'You're very quiet. Is anything wrong?' she asked.

He turned suddenly to look at her, and she recoiled when she saw that his eyes were full of anger.

'Wrong? I'll say there's something wrong! What's all this I hear about you and Peter? Wasn't I the idiot not to see it was you he was after. It's a wonder you haven't swanned off with him by now!'

'Colin! How can you say such a thing!'

'Can you deny it? Can you deny that

he's in love with you?'

'There was never anything between us,' she assured him, but her voice faltered as she remembered how she had responded to Peter's kisses, and Colin was quick to detect it.

'Are you telling me he never laid a finger on you?'

'He — he kissed me. Once. Just the one time after you and I had had a row,' she whispered miserably. 'After that he thought it was best to leave the farm.'

'He wouldn't have left, just like that, if there hadn't been more to it. Are you trying to tell me that a man like Barclay would stop at a kiss? And that you didn't encourage him?'

Pride rose in her at the scathing note in his voice.

'I'm sorry you feel you need to ask me these questions, Colin,' she said quietly and with the utmost dignity, and then, as he opened his mouth to speak, 'As far as I'm concerned, you've said quite enough. If you can't trust me, our marriage is finished.

'I'm going to Hazel's room,' she went on. 'I — I don't want to stay here tonight.'

*   *   *

Hazel carried her final box of ornaments up to her flat and set it down on the small kitchen table. Already she had made the place look comfortable and inviting, though it was strange to see so many familiar objects in such a different setting.

It had been the same when her father had driven her up to Kilgordon to see his new home, where a kindly, middle-aged woman was helping to keep house for him and Uncle Laurie.

The two men seemed happy with the fish farm they'd bought, and already her father was looking happier and much more relaxed now that he had left behind the pressure of working for Carmichael's. His health was sure to improve now, too.

Hazel was considering all this as she

gently unpacked her choice from the lovely ornaments collection which had been her mother's pride and joy. She knew she should be feeling warm and excited by the prospect of making her own future, but instead, the loneliness of her life seemed to press all around her.

She heard the door open and Tony's voice calling to her, but she made no move as she watched him walking slowly into the room. It was as if a spell had been cast upon her. As a shaft of sunlight fell on his face, it seemed to Hazel that she was seeing Tony for the first time.

She had never really looked at him properly, at his lop-sided grin and the humour in his eyes, although that humour was fast being displaced by puzzlement.

'Hazel?' he said hesitantly.

Her eyes still fixed on his, she slowly rose to her feet, and a moment later they were in each other's arms. Her eyes were brimming, but Tony was kissing her tears away.

Hazel felt a rush of joy at his touch . . . and suddenly realised she loved him — she had always loved him.

'Oh, sweetheart, it'll be all right,' he was murmuring. 'I'll look after you. Let me take care of you . . . '

'Oh, Tony, yes please,' she whispered, so softly that he barely heard her, and hardly dared believe what he'd thought he'd heard.

He took her face gently in his hands and looked into her eyes.

'You mean that?' he asked wonderingly. 'You really mean it?'

'Yes, I do.' She nodded and nestled closer into his arms. 'I love you, Tony.'

'And you'll marry me? You love me enough for that?' he persisted.

'Oh, Tony, of course I do. I don't know why I didn't realise it before.'

'Oh, Hazel, my love . . . We'll be so happy . . . '

'I can't imagine being any happier than I am right now,' she said with a contented sigh.

★ ★ ★

Leila Sutherland had pulled herself together in the days since she had unburdened her heart to Daniel.

At first, she had watched him with trepidation, waiting for some delayed reaction, but nothing seemed to happen and after a short while her pride once again rose up and she reverted to living her usual busy life.

One afternoon she found him waiting for her after she returned from her stint behind the counter at the local Oxfam shop.

Daniel had been through mental torture since Leila's bombshell. At first he hadn't wanted to be near her, could hardly bear to even be in the same room. But slowly that feeling had passed and now he felt only a deep sorrow.

He had gone to meet some of his friends for a lunchtime drink and, as he'd walked home past the jeweller's, his feet had slowed and he'd stared in the window at the pretty brooch he had mentally selected as a gift for Leila to celebrate their twenty-eighth wedding anniversary.

Twenty-eight years! It would be a great chunk to throw away because of the events of one night . . .

Of course, Leila wanted to hold on to their marriage. She'd told him that, and that she still loved him. And he still loved her.

It would take a long time to heal the hurt, but he knew he must try.

Hesitantly, he'd pushed open the heavy door of the jeweller's, and gone in to buy the brooch.

Now he had set their small table for two with candles and a bottle of wine, ready for supper that evening.

'At first I thought we'd go out to dinner,' he told her, 'but then I decided it would be nice to stay in. We should talk, Leila, though I'll say my piece quite quickly.

'I think we should both quietly put Robert Chisholm out of our lives.

What's done is done and all that matters is that I still love you, my darling.'

Leila came into his arms and he stroked her hair lovingly.

'I love you, too, Daniel,' she told him. 'I didn't realise how much until I thought I had lost you.'

Daniel held her close and for several moments they just enjoyed the renewed harmony between them.

'There is just one thing,' he said later, after they had eaten their supper. 'Weren't you consulting Chisholm about some sort of grant for Colin?'

'Yes. Apparently he had managed to work something out, but I wouldn't accept it. Anyway, Colin will sort himself out,' she said confidently. 'But I'll go to see him and Susan at Westgate soon to see how they're getting on.'

'I'll come with you,' Daniel offered. 'We're going to do as much as possible together from now on.'

★ ★ ★

Susan was smiling broadly as she put down the receiver after Hazel's excited phone call telling her about her engagement to Tony. She was delighted for her sister.

Hazel would be happy with Tony, she knew. He was doing well with his paintings, and he would encourage Hazel to work at her own art, too. She would be loved and respected by him — yes, she was a lucky girl.

Susan gave a disconsolate sigh. The past few days with Colin had convinced her that her own marriage was over, and that she had no alternative but to leave him.

She'd even got as far as deciding that she'd go to visit her Aunt Chrissie at Carleven for a few days, and make her plans from there.

When she told Mrs Campbell she was going away, the old lady eyed her closely, noticing that the girl had taken her largest case from the hall closet.

Shrewd woman that she was, she realised in a flash that Susan was leaving Colin!

Upstairs, Susan packed her case almost feverishly, taking advantage of the fact that Colin was out. She had phoned for a taxi to take her to the station and it would be here soon.

Suddenly she heard Colin's heavy footsteps downstairs and her heart sank. Now there was no way she could leave without having yet another scene with him.

'Susan? Are you upstairs? Susan!'

She heard him running up the stairs, then the door of their bedroom was thrown open.

'Susan, it's — what are you doing?' he demanded roughly. 'Well, never mind that — you'd better come downstairs. It's Gran — she's taken ill.'

Mrs Campbell was lying back in her chair, her face as white as parchment as she gasped for breath.

Susan took one look at her and turned to Colin.

'You'd better phone for the doctor.'

It seemed an eternity before Dr Craig arrived, but he quickly examined Mrs Campbell, then turned to Colin and Susan, waiting anxiously nearby.

'I'd say she's been overdoing things a bit, but a few days of bed-rest should see her right.'

'Oh, what a relief!' gasped Susan.

She was beginning to realise how much she had come to love Colin's grandmother. Now everything else must be put aside until Mrs Campbell was better again.

As they heard a car draw up outside, Susan suddenly remembered the taxi she had ordered.

'I — I'll go — it's probably just someone looking for directions,' she dissembled. Colin mustn't know she had been on the point of leaving.

Later in the evening, however, when she went upstairs to go to bed, she was confronted by Colin in their bedroom.

'What's all this?' he demanded, pointing at her case. 'Where were you planning on going? To see Peter Barclay?' he finished harshly.

Colour flew to her cheeks and her eyes sparkled with anger. How dare he suspect her of that?

'Think what you like,' she told him proudly. 'I don't care any more.'

She grabbed the case and took it through to the room Hazel had occupied, banging the door quickly behind her so that he would not see the hot tears of distress that had rushed to her eyes.

Colin stared after her, the pain in his heart so great that it was a constant ache now. What had happened to them? How had it all gone so wrong?

* * *

Leila rang Westgate next morning and couldn't mistake the heartfelt relief in Susan's voice when she answered the phone.

'Have you been worrying about me?' she asked. 'Well, worry no more! I took

269

your advice and talked to Daniel, and I'm pleased to say everything's fine between us now, though I won't pretend it was easy. Anyway, I wanted to see you to thank you.'

'I'm so glad . . . ' Susan felt relief flood through her. At least something was going right.

'We were thinking of coming to see you later,' Leila went on, and Susan leapt on the suggestion.

'I was going to ask if you would. Your mother's not been so well. Nothing serious — just overdoing things, the doctor said. But she'd be really pleased to see you. Why don't you come this afternoon and stay for a couple of days?' she finished, and so it was quickly arranged.

Leila and Daniel arrived at Westgate in the late afternoon, and although both Colin and Susan were there to greet them, Leila's sharp eyes soon detected that all was not well between them.

In marked contrast, Mrs Campbell was looking a great deal better as she sat up in bed and smiled with pleasure at seeing her daughter.

'What's wrong between Susan and Colin?' Leila asked. 'You could cut the atmosphere round here with a knife!'

'I know.' Mrs Campbell shook her head sadly. 'It seems that young Peter Barclay took a bit of a fancy to Susan — and Colin got wind of it and he's jealous.'

'You don't mean . . . ?' Leila began.

'Oh, no, there was nothing on Susan's side, I'm sure of that. The whole thing just brewed up because — well, the lass has been trying so hard to learn the ropes around here, and you know Colin — he's not the most patient lad. Never was! And he's been terribly on edge, what with the money worries and everything.'

'I'll have a word with him,' Leila promised. 'See what I can do.'

It was the following morning before she managed to corner him in the small room he used as a study. She followed him in and shut the door firmly behind her.

'I want to talk to you,' she said briskly. 'I want to ask what's gone wrong between you and Susan.'

His face grew hot with colour.

'Well, there's obviously no point in denying anything, is there?'

He shrugged. 'The truth is, she's just not happy here. She was turning to Peter Barclay, away from me. She told me herself that ... ' He paused, shaking his head.

'What did she tell you?'

'That she let him kiss her. How do I know it stopped there?'

'Is that what she told you?' demanded his mother.

'Well...yes...' he admitted grudgingly.

'Then it's the truth. Susan couldn't hide anything from you. I expect she's very hurt that you should even suspect her of being unfaithful. And I can't say I blame her!'

'Maybe. But she really isn't happy here, Mum. I can't give her the things she needs.'

'You can give her your love. I'd be very surprised if she puts material things higher than that. Do you still love her?'

'Of course I do.' His eyes were tortured.

'Then tell her!' She took his hand. 'Isn't she worth fighting for?'

Suddenly his eyes filled with tears as all the pressures that had been tormenting him finally pushed him to breaking point.

'Don't worry about it any more,' his mother said soothingly. 'Go and talk to her — now.'

Susan was upstairs in their bedroom, changing out of her jeans before they all gathered together for a meal.

As he closed the door behind him, she looked up at him, her face pale and afraid, and his heart contracted. Had he done this to her?

He wanted to say so much, to try to make her understand, but he couldn't find the words. Instead he held out his arms.

'Can you ever forgive me?' he asked in a voice that laid bare every shred of his distress.

Susan's face lit up as though touched by a sunbeam and a moment later she was in his arms, soft, healing tears rolling down her cheeks.

'Oh, Colin . . . I love you, only you!'

Then he was kissing her fiercely, with all the longing that had been suppressed by anxiety over the last few tortured weeks.

Susan wound her arms around his neck, surrendering to the passion. It was wonderful to be in his arms once more and to know that their love was as strong and all-consuming as ever.

⋆ ⋆ ⋆

Leila and Daniel spent several happy days on the farm. But before they left, Leila had another long talk with her mother.

'What about that mortgage for Colin, Mum?' she asked bluntly. 'He needs support from the bank and the mortgage is the only way he can get it.

'Times have changed, you know. I know the farm was always prosperous before, and that's the way you remember it, but it's in serious trouble now.

'Colin's clever — he can pull it round — but he needs support and he's not going to get it any other way. If you sign the papers, he has a chance of paying it all back in a year or two. Otherwise, you'll lose the farm.'

'I just can't believe — ' Mrs Campbell began.

Sensing a further argument, Leila played the only card left to her.

'Did it ever occur to you that you might have contributed to the trouble between Colin and Susan? If he hadn't been so harassed with money worries, he would have had more time for her.'

Mrs Campbell looked stricken.

'I never thought of it like that,' she whispered, then, 'Send the boy in to talk to me,' she told Leila gruffly. 'I want to know everything. And then — I'll sign.'

It was a long meeting, but when Colin emerged he was smiling, and already looked less like the weight of the world was resting on his shoulders.

As Leila and Daniel drove away that afternoon, she looked back to see Colin and Susan standing in the doorway, their arms entwined about one another, and smiled with satisfaction.

Daniel saw the smile.

'Colin told me what you did to help them,' he said, and reached out to cover her hand with his own. 'I'm very proud, my darling.'

'I've learned that happiness is very precious, Daniel,' she told him softly.

* * *

Hazel's wedding to Tony took place on a warm, bright day in April when the daffodils were in full bloom and the air was balmy after the harsh, cold winds of winter.

Leila was full of energy and enthusiasm as she and Susan helped Hazel to dress in her lovely oyster-satin bridal gown.

'You look like a princess,' Leila said sincerely. 'Doesn't she, Susan?'

'Beautiful — just beautiful!' whispered Susan emotionally. She could hardly believe this stunning vision was her own little sister.

There were gasps of admiration for the whole bridal party as they assembled at the back of the church, then began to walk slowly down the aisle.

Colin, standing beside Tony at the altar, turned his gaze upon Susan, radiant in pale primrose, and their eyes met in loving understanding.

Daniel glanced tenderly at his wife, and reached to clasp her hand in his.

And as Tony, waiting impatiently at the altar, turned to look at his bride, his heart swelled with pride and love as he looked forward to their shining future together.

'Dearly beloved . . .'

The deep voice of the minister sounded throughout the church, and his words found an echo in many loving hearts.

THE END

We do hope that you have enjoyed reading this large print book.

Did you know that all of our titles are available for purchase?

We publish a wide range of high quality large print books including:
Romances, Mysteries, Classics
General Fiction
Non Fiction and Westerns

Special interest titles available in large print are:
The Little Oxford Dictionary
Music Book, Song Book
Hymn Book, Service Book

Also available from us courtesy of Oxford University Press:
Young Readers' Dictionary
(large print edition)
Young Readers' Thesaurus
(large print edition)

For further information or a free brochure, please contact us at:
Ulverscroft Large Print Books Ltd.,
The Green, Bradgate Road, Anstey,
Leicester, LE7 7FU, England.
Tel: (00 44) **0116 236 4325**
Fax: (00 44) **0116 234 0205**

THREE TALL TAMARISKS

Christine Briscomb

Joanna Baxter flies from Sydney to run her parents' small farm in the Adelaide Hills while they recover from a road accident. But after crossing swords with Riley Kemp, life is anything but uneventful. Gradually she discovers that Riley's passionate nature and quirky sense of humour are capturing her emotions, but a magical day spent with him on the coast comes to an abrupt end when the elegant Greta intervenes. Did Riley love Greta after all?

SUMMER IN HANOVER SQUARE

Charlotte Grey

The impoverished Margaret Lambart is suddenly flung into all the glitter of the Season in Regency London. Suspected by her godmother's nephew, the influential Marquis St. George, of being merely a common adventuress, she has, nevertheless, a brilliant success, and attracts the attentions of the young Duke of Oxford. However, when the Marquis discovers that Margaret is far from wanting a husband he finds he has to revise his estimate of her true worth.

CONFLICT OF HEARTS

Gillian Kaye

Somerset, at the end of World War I: Daniel Holley, unhappily married to an ailing wife and father of four grown-up children, is attracted to beautiful schoolteacher Harriet Bray, but he knows his love is hopeless. Daniel's only daughter, Amy, who dreams of becoming a milliner and is caught up in her love for young bank clerk John Tottle, looks on as the drama of Daniel and Harriet's fate and happiness gradually unfolds.